David Bartlett

The life of Lady Jane Grey

David Bartlett

The life of Lady Jane Grey

ISBN/EAN: 9783337118921

Printed in Europe, USA, Canada, Australia, Japan

Cover: Foto ©Raphael Reischuk / pixelio.de

More available books at **www.hansebooks.com**

THE LIFE

OF

LADY JANE GREY.

BY

DAVID W. BARTLETT.

TO MY MOTHER,

THIS

LITTLE VOLUME

IS

Most affectionately Inscribed.

PREFACE.

I OFFER no apology for preparing this volume. The lovely woman who is its subject, possessed a character worthy of contemplation. Her career is one of the most interesting and tragical to be found in the pages of English history.

But I apologise most heartily for the manner in which I have executed my task, though apologies are not generally accepted by the reading public. My object has been to prepare a popular sketch of the Life of Lady Jane Grey—to make a book so convenient in size, and simple in style, as to command the attention of the million. The subject of this memoir existed so long ago, that it has been impossible to discover any new facts connected with her life; but I have searched thoroughly all the proper authorities, and present, in a single volume, everything of interest which has reference to Lady Jane

It has seemed to me necessary to give a brief sketch of the times immediately previous to those in which Lady Jane Grey existed, for her own career and sad fate were, in a manner, dependent upon the political events of those times. Her claim to the throne of England cannot be understood, without adverting to the history of Henry VIII. and his queens, one of whom was the dearest female friend Lady Jane ever possessed.

My authorities in the preparation of this volume have been, Knight, Goldsmith, Hume, Fox, Burnet, Agnes Strickland, and Speed. I am also much indebted to an English volume upon Lady Jane Grey, by Howard.

I shall be content with little praise for my book, if any of those who read it shall be led to imitate the character of the beautiful and illustrious woman whose sad, yet in another sense glorious, career, it records.   D. W. B.

Hartford, Conn.,

CONTENTS.

CHAPTER I.

CHAPTER II.

CHAPTER III.

a

CHAPTER IV.

CHAPTER V.

CHAPTER VI.

CHAPTER VII.

CHAPTER XII.

CHAPTER XIII.

LIFE OF LADY JANE GREY.

CHAPTER I.

LADY JANE GREY was born in Bradgate, Leicestershire, one of the interior counties of England. The precise date of her birth cannot be satisfactorily ascertained, no two of the chroniclers of her times agreeing upon this point. The probabilities are, however, that she was born in the year 1537, being of the same age as Edward VI., with whose fate in after years her own fortunes were closely connected.

The family of GREY was originally of Norman extraction. Rollo or Frilburt was the first of the family record; he was chamberlain to Robert, Duke of Normandy, who made him a present of the castle and lands of Croy, in Picardy, from which sprung the name de Croy, and subsequently de Grey.

John, Lord de Croy, only son of Rollo, married Adela, daughter and co-heir of William Fitz Osbert, by whom he had a son—

Sir Arnold de Grey, who soon after the Norman conquest became lord of Water Eaton, Stoke, and Rotherfield. By his wife Joan, heiress of the Baron Ponte del Arche, he had a son—

Auchitel de Grey, whose eldest son's name was—

Richard de Grey, whose son—

Auchitel de Grey, married Eva, daughter of Baldwin de Redrers, Earl of Devon. Their eldest son's name was—

John de Grey—his son—

Henry de Grey had a grant of the lands of Thurrock, in Essex, from Richard I. His second son—

John de Grey, had a high position under the government. He married Emma, daughter and heiress of Geoffrey de Glanville—their son—

Reginald de Grey, married Maud, daughter of the Baron of Willon. Their son—

John de Grey, married the daughter of Lord Basset of Drayton. Their son—

Roger de Grey, married Elizabeth, daughter of Lord Hastings. Their son—

Reginald de Grey, married Eleanor, daughter of Lord Straise. He commanded all the king's castles in Wales, in the reign of Edward III. Their son—

Reginald de Grey, married Joan, daughter of Lord Ashley. Their son—

Sir Edward de Grey, married Elizabeth, daughter of Lord Ferrens. Their son—

Sir John Grey married the eldest daughter of the Earl of Rivers—she after his death marrying King Edward IV. Their son—

Sir Thomas Grey held high office under Henry VII.—was created Knight of the Garter, Earl of Huntingdon and Marquis of Dorset. His son—

Thomas Grey, the second Marquis of Dorset, was a great favorite of Henry VIII., in the third year of whose reign he was general of the army sent into Spain for the purpose of invading Guienne. Peace was restored, and two years after the, with four of his brothers, the Duke of

Suffolk and others, went to Paris, and obtained great renown at the tournaments of St. Denis. In 1520, he was present at the interview between Henry VIII. and the French monarch Francis, at the famous *Champ d'Or*, or Field of Gold. He had the honor of carrying the sword of state on this occasion, and won renown at the tournaments which graced the distinguished meeting of the monarchs.

In 1522, he was chosen to go to Calais to receive and escort the Emperor Charles V. into England. He married for a second wife, Margaret, daughter of Sir Robert Wotton. He was a man of extraordinary abilities, of exceedingly studious disposition, and was not characterized by the vices of his age. Some of his wise sayings—for he was fond of writing—are preserved to this day in the libraries of English antiquarians. We will quote a specimen.

"The greatest trust between man and man is giving counsel."

"Never was the man merry who had more than one woman in his bed, one friend in his bosom, one faith in his heart."

His son—

Henry Grey, third Marquis of Dorset, came to

the title in 1530   He was father to LADY JANE
GREY. He was at first Constable of England,
and possessed other high trusts under the gov-
ernment, and finally received the title of his
wife's father—the Duke of Suffolk. He married
Frances, eldest daughter of Charles Brandon,
Duke of Suffolk, whose wife was sister to Henry
VIII. The children of Henry, third Marquis of
Dorset (afterwards Duke of Suffolk), were Jane,
Katharine, and Mary. It was through the mar-
riage of Henry, third Marquis of Dorset, that the
claim to the crown of England came into the
Dorset family.

Lady Jane Grey's claim to the crown was
through her mother, and it will be necessary for
us to give a brief sketch of her descent upon the
mother's side.

Henry VII., one of the wisest kings of England, married Elizabeth of York, and their children were Arthur, Margaret, Henry, Mary and
Katherine. Of these only three survived their
parents—Margaret, afterward Queen of Scotland,
Henry, King of England, and Mary, who became
Queen of France.

Mary Tudor, the grandmother of Lady Jane
Grey, was born in the year 1498, and was a great

favorite with her brother, the terrible Henry
VIII. She was very beautiful, and won the
heart of the Duke of Suffolk. Charles Brandon,
Duke of Suffolk, was a person of elegant appearance, most winning manners and exalted courage.
He was perhaps the most accomplished gentleman
of his time, and contrived to win the affections
of the king, who made him an esquire of his
body, and chamberlain of the principality of
Wales. He fought a battle with the French off
Brest, and the following year asked leave to attend the expedition to Terouenne and Tournay.
Henry appointed him to the command of the
vanguard of the army, and also made him Viscount l'Isle. The next year he also made him
Duke of Suffolk. The duke was fascinated by
the youthful graces of Mary Tudor, and she was
pleased with his elegant manners, handsome appearance and courageous actions. Their love,
however, was probably unknown to the king.
At any rate, in 1514, Mary was married to Louis
XII. of France. The French monarch when in
the prime of life was tall, agile and handsome,
was somewhat dissipated in his youth, but upon
his accession to the throne, he forsook his vices
He had been compelled by Louis XI. to marry

his daughter Jeanne, a deformed girl, but of amiable disposition. The poor girl loved her handsome husband passionately, but when he came to the throne, he put her away through a dispensation of the pope. Jeanne wept and begged in vain, for Louis married Anne of Brittany, who was a faithful and pious wife. She died in January, 1514. Mary, the sister of Henry VIII., was affianced to Prince Charles, grandson of Maximilian and Ferdinand, while his father was detained years before at Windsor Castle. The prince did not consider the engagement binding, and Louis XII. proposed the hand of his own daughter to him as his wife. Henry VIII. was frantic with rage at what he termed the treachery of the prince, and the ambassador of France proposed, with adroitness, that Mary Tudor should marry the king, his master. Henry accepted the proposal—never for a moment considering the heart of his sister. The French king was fifty-three years old while Mary was only sixteen, and very charming in her beauty. She was deeply in love with Charles Brandon, but saw that opposition was utterly useless, and consented to the union. A treaty was made between the two monarchs, Louis agree-

ing to pay Henry a million of crowns in ten
yearly instalments, in discharge of arrears due
on the old treaty of Etaples, and Henry bound
himself to give his sister Mary a dower of four
hundred thousand crowns.   A marriage ceremony took place at Greenwich, on the 7th of
August, the French ambassador acting as proxy
for the king.   Louis became very impatient for
the personal society of his beautiful wife, but she,
her heart far from being his, preferred to linger
in England.   Louis wrote to Cardinal Wolsey
early in September, demanding that Mary come
over to France at once, but she staid at her
brother's court till October, when the court re-
moved with her to Dover, on the coast, where
with a gorgeous retinue she sailed for Boulogne.
Among her retinue was her lover Charles Brandon, and one of her maids of honor, was the then
young and pretty Anne Boleyn, who afterwards
became the wife of Henry VIII., and ended her
brilliant but sad career upon the scaffold.   Lady
Anne Grey and Elizabeth Grey, sisters to the
Marquis of Dorset, were also among the young
queen's maids of honor.

   The royal company had been detained at Dover on account of the fearful storms which swept

over the channel, but on the second day of October, Henry conducted his sister to the shore, kissed her affectionately, and committed her to God and the king, her future lord. The sea was yet violently agitated, and the perils of the short voyage were great,—the fleet being scattered, and some of the ships driven upon the French shore. On the way from Boulogne to Abbeville, Queen Mary rode on a palfrey which was covered with a golden cloth, and her ladies were dressed in crimson velvet. On the 8th of October the French monarch received her joyfully at Abbeville, and the day after they were re-married. The day was one of great festivity and splendor, but the next morning the queen was severely tried by an order of Louis, to the effect that all her English attendants should return home. Two or three exceptions were finally made, and the Duke of Suffolk, the queen's old lover, remained in the quality of ambassador. The queen's coronation took place on the 5th of November, and there followed it a continual round of festivities. Louis seemed to be intoxicated with his charming young wife, and indulged in dangerous dissipations. In the meantime, the Duke of Suffolk remained at the French court, though his conduct

towards Mary was irreproachable. On the first of
January, Louis, worn out with his excesses, expired at Paris. Ten days only after his death,
Mary wrote the following letter to Cardinal Wolsey, showing pretty plainly that her heart was
not broken by the death of her royal husband:

"My reverend, good Lord,—I recommend me
to you, and thank you for letters and good lessons that you have given to me. My lord, I pray
you as my trust is in you, to remember me to
the king, my brother, for such cause and business
as I have for to do: for as now I have no other
to put my trust in but the king my brother, and
you. And as it shall please the king my brother
and his council, I will be ordered; and so pray
I you, my lord, to show his grace, saying that
the king my husband is departed to God, whose
soul God pardon. And whereas you advise me
that I should make no promise, my lord, I trust
the king my brother and you will not depend on
me solely please God. I trust I have so ordered
myself since I came hither, that it hath been to
the honor of the king my brother and me, since
I came hither, and so I trust to continue. If there
be anything that I may do for you, I would be

glad for to do it in these parts, and shall be glad
to do it for you. No more to you at this time,
but God preserve you.

"Written at Paris the 10 of January, 1515,

"By your loving friend,

"MARY, Queen of France."

A short time after the date of this letter, Mary
wrote a letter to Henry, begging him to send for
her, as she longed to see his face. The truth was,
she longed to see the face of her old lover, the
Duke of Suffolk, who had returned a short time
before Louis's death, to England. Henry, in answer to his sister's letter, sent the Duke of Suffolk and others to Paris, to escort her home. As
soon as she met Suffolk, Mary was in transports
of joy; and he, being encouraged by her, ventured upon asking for her hand. She replied
that if he did not win her in a month, he would
never do so. They were soon privately married
in Paris, after which Mary wrote the king, her
brother, imploring his pardon for the step she
had taken without his leave. They then travelled
to Calais, at which place her marriage was celebrated by public rites and ceremonies.

Henry was angry for a time, and when the

couple returned to England, they were afraid to
come up to court, but went to their seat in Suffolk. From that place Mary wrote another letter
to the king, who, loving both her and his old favorite, the duke, consented to a reconciliation.
By certain persons, the marriage was said to be
illegal, as the Duke of Suffolk's first wife, Lady
Mortimer, was still alive; but she had been repudiated by him long before. After his marriage
the duke frequented the court, and was a favorite
of the king. A year after the marriage, Margaret, Queen of Scots, came to London, and the
king and his two sisters had a happy meeting.

Henry, the third Marquis of Dorset, married
Frances, the daughter of the Duke of Suffolk.
Their eldest child was the Lady Jane Grey, and
in many things the Marquis of Dorset was
scarcely worthy to be the parent of so good, so
illustrious a daughter. His mother complained
bitterly of his treatment of her, declaring that he
withheld her property from her, and in other
matters conducted himself in a most undutiful
manner. The family coat-of-arms is thus de-
scribed: Barry of six, argent and azure; in chief,
three torteauxex, ermine: the motto, *A ma puis-
sance.*

CHAPTER II.

IN order to clearly understand the causes which
led to Lady Jane Grey's innocent usurpation of
the English crown, it will be necessary briefly to
sketch the history of the Protestant Reformation
in England, and therefore to go back to the com-
mencement of Henry VIII.'s reign.   That prince
was in his eighteenth year when he ascended the
throne, made vacant by his father's death.   He
was exceedingly handsome, frank and generous
in his disposition at this time, though noted for
his ardent love of pleasure, and he was a universal favorite.   Previous to his coronation,
Henry had been married to Katharine of Arragon, the daughter of Queen Isabella of Spain, and

B

the widow of Prince Arthur, who was the eldest son of Henry VII., and brother to Henry VIII. Prince Arthur and Katharine were married in November, 1501, the former fifteen years of age —the latter seventeen. Five months after the marriage, Prince Arthur died, and Katharine was left a young widow. Her marriage-portion consisted of 200,000 crowns, and half the sum had been paid at the time of the marriage. Her father and mother now signified their wish for the return of their daughter with her marriage-portion. Henry VII., to do away with the necessity of returning so much money, and to gain the unpaid portion of the young widow's dower, immediately proposed that she should marry her brother-in-law, Prince Henry. But Henry was five years younger than Katharine, and the proposed match was distasteful to him; nevertheless, in June 1503, she was betrothed to him. Three years later, Henry VII. conceived a strong desire to marry Joanna, the sister of Katharine; and fearing that the people would not be satisfied with the marriage of the father and two sons into one family, he forced Prince Henry the day before he attained his fifteenth year, to solemnly protest against his betrothment to Katharine.

But so soon as the young prince was forbidden
to think of marriage with Katharine, he at once
was determined to obtain her, and they were
carefully kept apart to prevent a private marriage. When at length the king became convinced of the hopeless insanity of Joanna, Prince
Henry and Katharine were married. The event
took place on the 11th of June, 1509, and they
were together crowned on the 24th of the same
month. The queen at this time, though five
years older than the king, was, if not handsome,
at least of pleasing appearance, and possessed a
pious heart and beautiful disposition. She was
fond of reading pious books, and all her pleasures were of the gentler sort. That Henry had
great confidence in her during the early part of
his reign, is very evident from the momentous
trusts which he at different times reposed in her.
At the close of 1510, the queen gave birth to an
infant son, which was christened Henry, but
which died a few weeks after its advent into the
world. Had this child lived, the queen probably would have been saved all her future troubles. In November, 1514, Katharine again became a mother to a prince, which survived but a
few days. In February, 1816, was born the

Princess Mary, who was destined in later years to bear so cruel a sway over the fortunes of the illustrious lady who is the subject of this work. Katharine bore Henry five children, but one, of them all, arriving to years of maturity.

When Henry VIII. came to the throne of England, the religion of the country was Roman Catholic. Indeed, the great Reformation was not commenced. A long time before, Wycliffe had denounced the abominations of the Romish Church, but his doctrines had not taken root in 'he popular mind, though unquestionably there were many pious people in England who at the date of Henry's accession to power, were dis-gusted with many of the practices of the Romish priests. Eight years later, and Martin Luther, the humble monk, sounded the note of alarm over Europe, against the frightful doctrine of indulgences. As yet, on every other point, he was a good Catholic; but soon, with an intellect made clear and strong through liberty and a freedom from the prevailing superstition of the times, he went still further, and even questioned the supremacy of the Pope. Germany at once was made the theatre of intense excitement, through the fearless and eloquent words of the courageous

monk; and though the most persevering and en-
ergetic efforts were made to put down Luther
and his heretical opinions, through the providence of God they were unavailing.

The noise of the excitement on the Continent
was heard in England, and Henry VIII. turned
author in defence of his religion. He wrote a
book to confute the heresies of Luther, entitled
"Defence of the Seven Sacraments against Martin Luther," a copy of which was sent to Pope
Leo, who was so pleased, that he granted to
Henry the title of "Defender of the Faith." Luther immediately replied to the royal author,
scattering his flimsy arguments to the winds, and
treating him in any but a reverential manner.
He even affected not to believe Henry wrote the
book, and this piqued the monarch more than
Luther's logic. By the skilful management of
Cardinal Wolsey, the whole affair set the king
the more firmly against Lutheranism, and a con-
temptible persecution was at once commenced
against all persons who possessed copies of the
heretical books.

Thomas Wolsey was the son of an Ipswich
butcher, who gave him an admirable education,
and fitted him for the Church. He was first a

country parson, but his learning, wit, and talents
becoming known to Bishop Fox, he introduced
him to his master, Henry VII. Upon the accession of Henry VIII. Bishop Fox and the Duke
of Norfolk struggled for the supremacy in the
council, and when the bishop perceived that the
soldier was fast gaining the confidence of the
king, he brought Wolsey under the notice of
Henry, hoping thereby to get the upper hand of
the Duke of Norfolk. But Wolsey, with aston-
ishing talent, became himself the most powerful
and influential man at court, and left his friends
the duke and bishop, far behind him in the race
for distinction. He at once adapted himself to
all the sensual desires of the king, eating and
drinking like any courtier, and yet when there
was occasion, showing that he possessed not only
profound learning, but also great abilities as a
statesman. He was made lord chancellor of the
kingdom, and was appointed by the pope to the
lucrative and exalted office of papal legate. He
now became the most gorgeous prelate the world
ever saw, maintaining a train of eight hundred
persons, and at one time receiving an income as
large as that of the king. He was the patron of
learning and the arts, and was popular with the

people until he was obliged, to meet the wants of Henry, to tax them too oppressively. Throughout his most brilliant career he was devoted to the interests of his king. He did not hesitate to minister to his basest passions, though this was done for the security of his own interests. He was constantly aspiring to the papal chair, and made everything but his devotion to Henry, bend to this ambitious desire. He concealed from the nation his selfishness for a time, but by repeated taxes he lost his popularity. He built the famous palace at Hampton Court, which stands to this day a monument to his splendor. After it was finished, Henry asked of him who it was intended for · whereupon the great prelate, fearing the jealousy of the terrible monarch, (for the palace was the most sumptuous then built in the kingdom,) very handsomely gave it to Henry.

But England was fast approaching the hour ever reckoned the most important in her religious history, and Wolsey, his sad fate. The king had long been noted for his intrigues, his gross devotion to sensual pleasures, and his inconstancy, but had treated his wife with a certain respect, which even that coarse age demanded from him as consistent with propriety. In the year 1523,

he fell in love with Anne Boleyn, the daughter
of Sir Thomas Boleyn. She was twenty years
of age, tall and slender, with dark hair and brilliant eyes, and very fascinating manners. Previous to seeing her Henry had indulged in a love
or fancy for her sister Mary Boleyn, indeed some
of the chroniclers of that age declare that she
was his mistress, which, upon the whole, we do
not believe. Anne was sprightly, witty, and
possessed of a large share of animal beauty, and
well calculated to excite the gross passions of the
king. He first met her in her father's garden,
at Hever, by accident, and being surprised and
delighted with her beauty entered into a conversation with her, and was still more surprised and
delighted with her wit. When he next saw
Wolsey he said, that "he had been discoursing
with a young lady who had the wit of an angel
and was worthy of a crown;" most prophetic
words! "It is sufficient," replied the acute Wolsey, "if your majesty finds her worthy of your
love." The prelate was quite willing that the
king should become engrossed in another love-
affair, having no doubt but it would end like all
his intrigues in the ruin of his victim, consequently he suggested that Anne be appointed

maid of honor to the queen. As a matter of course, Anne Boleyn, being the most beautiful and accomplished woman at court, soon was sur-rounded with admirers. Lord Henry Percy, son of the Earl of Northumberland, though contract-ed by his father to the daughter of the Earl of Shrewsbury, fell violently in love with Anne, and she so far returned his passion as to private-ly engage herself to him. Indeed there can be no possible question about the sincerity of her love for Percy, and she never loved any one else. The cardinal was so blind as not to see the affec-tion which the young couple entertained for each other, and Henry himself first made the discov-ery, and from the jealousy which at once filled his heart, discovered further that he himself loved the beautiful Anne.

He at once charged Wolsey to separate the lovers and to dissolve their engagement. Percy and Anne were both plunged into grief, for as yet the latter had not indulged in visions of am-bition and power. The cardinal sent for Percy and reprimanded him severely for his secret en-gagement with Anne, and he was shortly after banished from court, and compelled to marry the daughter of the Earl of Shrewsbury. He was a

b
3

man of gentle manners, of noble affections, and his sad fortune completely wrecked his happiness. That he never fully recovered from his bitter loss is very evident from the history of his subsequent career. Anne was dismissed to her father's house, being very much offended and vowing that if it ever were in her power, she would be revenged on Wolsey. At this time she had little idea how soon would come the day on which she would take ample revenge upon the cardinal. After a little time, however, the king came down to her father's castle, but Anne would not see him. Shortly after, to soften her heart, Henry advanced her father to the peerage under the title of Viscount Rochford. In 1527, Anne again appeared at court, and Henry endeavored in vain to seduce her from the path of virtue. To his criminal addresses, she replied,

"Most noble king, I will rather lose my life than my virtue, which will be the greatest and best part of the dowry I shall bring my husband."

"I shall continue to hope," replied the king.

"I understand not," she said, "how you should retain such hope. Your wife I cannot be, both in respect of mine own unworthiness, and also because you have a queen already. Your mistress I will not be."

Henry was the more deeply set upon obtaining Anne, now that there seemed little hope for success. He wrote her a series of love-letters filled with passion and a half-sensual love. That Anne replied to some of these letters cannot be denied, and it is evident that about this time she began to dream of a brilliant career at court. It is not proper from this date to call her a virtuous woman, for whether or not she consented to the king's desires, she *did* receive not only his addresses but those of another married man—Sir Thomas Wyatt. No woman of a pure heart would ever for a moment carry on an intrigue with a married man, and the only reason why Anne now refused to become the royal mistress was her hope of eventually becoming his wife. For now Henry began to pretend that his conscience was troubled because of his marriage with Katharine of Arragon. She had previously married his brother Arthur, and, therefore, his marriage was incestuous, he claimed. Though Katharine had been to him for seventeen years a most dutiful, and lovely, and pious wife, yet the royal hypocrite was now ready to cast her off on the score of conscience. There were also other and important reasons. The queen had borne him five children, but only one of the five, the Princess Mary, survived. Henry was naturally anxious to leave the crown to a male heir. Katharine was now growing old, and possessed little personal beauty, and the doctrines of Luther had been received with so much favor in England, that there was quite a party who were secretly in favor of Henry's divorce from Katharine, hoping that Anne Boleyn would favor the Reformation. Cardinal Wolsey also favored the idea of a divorce, but had not the slightest idea that Henry would ever marry Anne. The king now announced his determination to Cardinal Wolsey of marrying Anne Boleyn, and making her Queen of England. It is said that the cardinal was utterly astonished, and fell upon his knees before his generous but terrible master, and implored of him to renounce so perilous an idea. It may be that he felt already a presentiment of his fate, for he must have been well aware that he had made an enemy of Anne. Perceiving that the king was immovably fixed in his determination, he at once affected to acquiesce in it, and offered his services to bring it

about. And now began the dawn of the great
Reformation in England. For two years Henry
importuned the pope to grant a divorcement
from Katharine, but the pontiff, fearing Charles
who had an army at his gates, dared not grant
the wish of Henry. At length, he appointed a
commission, consisting of Campeggio and Wolsey
to examine the whole question. The two legates
opened their court, and the king and queen appeared before them. The king answered to his
name in a bold voice, but the queen said not a
word. When the citation was repeated she
threw herself upon her knees before the king,
and made in tears one of the most pathetic ap-
peals to his sense of justice. When she rose up
she walked slowly out of court, and when the
receiver-general upon whose arm she leant, said,
" Madam, you are called back ;" (for the crier
said, " Katharine, Queen of England, come again
into court ;") she replied, " I hear it well enough ;
but on––on––go you on, for this is no court
wherein I can have justice ; proceed, therefore."

Her appeal made a deep impression upon
those who heard it, and Henry arose and declared adroitly, that she had always been a gentle and virtuous wife, and that the wish for a

divorce was simply with him a matter of con·
science. Yet previous to this, he had not hesi-
tated to declare to those in his confidence that
the queen was deficient in all those qualities
which now he gave her credit for possessing.
Such was the duplicity of this blood-thirsty and
ravenous king. Henry felt almost sure of a ver-
dict in his favor, but Campeggio took the lead
and utterly refused to give judgment, referring
the whole matter to the pope. The Duke of
Suffolk was much enraged, and striking his fist
fiercely upon the table, declared that no good
had ever befallen England since cardinals came
there. He aimed his blow at Wolsey, who rose
and with lofty calmness replied to the insult,
among other things saying, " But for me, simple
cardinal as I am, you at this moment would have
no head upon your shoulders," referring to the
occasion when he had plead the cause of the
duke before the offended king. But from this
moment Wolsey's fate was sealed. Cranmer, an
eminent theologian, proposed that the king appeal to the universities of Europe—that the marriage be dissolved without asking leave of the
pope. This bold idea was well suited to Henry's
temperament and desires, and he at once re-

ceived Cranmer into favor, and a change was
soon perceptible in his affection for the Romish
religion. The introduction of any papal bull
into England was prohibited, and not long afterwards the parliament abolished the payment of
first-fruits to the court of Rome. The universities of Bologna and Paris pronounced Henry's
marriage with Katharine to be incestuous, but
Luther and the German universities utterly refused to sanction the divorce, Luther declaring
that he would sooner consent to Henry's marrying two wives than to his putting away Katharine to indulge his lust for Anne.

Annie now dissembled no more, but avowed
herself Wolsey's enemy, placing in the king's
hands copies of the letters of the cardinal to
Rome, which proved very clearly that Wolsey
was fully committed to the cause of the unfortunate Queen Katharine. Bills were soon filed
against him in the court of King's Bench, accus-
ing him of transgressing the laws of the land in
his capacity of pope's legate. The cardinal was
completely overcome, and offered at once to give
up the whole of his immense property, provided
he might retain his rank in the Church. The
king granted one interview with the prelate, but

it was the last. It is supposed that Anne ex
torted a promise from the monarch never to see
him again. He was banished to Esher, a quiet,
lonely, but beautiful place, but Wolsey, whose
whole life had been spent at court, who had been
really the head of the nation, pined away amid
the solitudes of the place. He was well aware
that Anne was determined upon his complete
ruin, for he said, "There is a *night-crow* that pos-
sesses the royal ear against me!" He was taken
violently ill, and the news reached the ear of
Henry. The monarch, iron-hearted as he was,
could not so soon forget the man who for many
years had been his dearest friend and counsellor,
and he therefore sent his physicians to the cardinal and also a ring with his image engraven
upon it. It was only a sickness of the heart after
all, for Wolsey upon receiving these tokens from
his monarch rapidly recovered. He came to Rich-
mond, very near to court, but Anne grew the
more determined to end his fortunes.

He became meek and humble, gave away his
income to the poor, and grew vastly popular with
the people. Indeed, it is a significant fact, that
through his whole career those persons who were
near the cardinal, in his household, or otherwise,

became strongly attached to him. He was ordered to proceed to York, within his archbish-
opric. On the 4th of November, 1529, while at
dinner Wolsey was arrested. The Earl of Northumberland drove up into the yard, and Wolsey
with a pleasant countenance, went out to meet
him, anticipating no harm. The earl was violently agitated, but laying his trembling hand upon
the old man's shoulder, said, " My lord, I arrest
you of high treason !" For a few moments the
cardinal stood silent, as if completely overcome,
and then he burst out into cries and lamentations.
He set out at once with the earl to go to his trial
and execution. At Sheffield Park, he was ill a
fortnight with the dysentery, and when he jour-
nied on, he was feeble and pale. The third
night he reached Leicester Abbey, and when the
monks received him, he said to the abbot,
"Father, I am come to lay my bones among
you." They carried him to the bed from
which he never rose. When he was dying,
he said to the lieutenant of the Tower, who had
his person in charge :

"Master Kingston, I pray you have me com-
mended most humbly to his majesty, and beseech
him, on my behalf, to call to his gracious remem

brance all matters that have passed between us
from the beginning, especially respecting Queen
Katharine and himself, and then shall his conscience know whether I have offended him or not.
He is a prince of most royal courage, and hath
a princely heart—for rather than miss or want
any part of his will, he will endanger one half of
his kingdom. And I do assure you I have often
kneeled before him in his privy-chamber, sometimes for three hours together, to persuade him
from his appetite, and could not prevail. And
Master Kingston, this I will say—had I but
served God as diligently as I served the king, he
would not have given me over in my gray hairs.
Howbeit, this is my just reward for my pains and
diligence, not regarding my service to God, but
only my duty to my prince."

Thus perished this gorgeous churchman, who
had so long been the glory of his church and his
country. When the news came to Henry of his
death, he manifested little sorrow—proving that
his heart was hard and cruel, and without feeling. Anne Boleyn's revengeful purpose was accomplished, and she now contented herself with
contemptuous treatment of the Queen Katharine.

At this time, Cromwell, the son of a black-

smith at Putney, came into favor with Henry.
He was a man of great talents, and was destined
to play an important part in the Reformation.
Cromwell not only advised the king to deny the
Pope, but to assert his own supremacy over the
Church. The convocations of York and Canterbury, declared the marriage null and void.
About this time Henry sent orders for Queen
Katharine to leave Windsor Castle. She retired
to her own estate at Ampthill, and never saw
the king again. Cranmer was made Archbishop
of Canterbury, and Henry was fully resolved
upon putting away Katharine, without the Pope's
consent. On the morning of the 25th of January,
1533, he was privately married to Anne, and a
few months after, Cranmer held an archiepisco-
pal court, and declared Katharine's marriage to
be null and void. Anne was crowned on a beautiful day—the first of June—amid splendors and
pageants, and thus at last she stood in that brilliant but dangerous position, which she had been
longing for so many years. She was Queen of
England! She had cast beneath her feet the
neck of the proudest prelate England ever saw.
She had walked right royally over the heart of
a poor, persecuted woman, the daughter and wife

of a king: and now was at the summit of her fortunes! But already the throne upon which she sat began to tremble—already the grim monarch whom she pretended to love, was losing his passion for her, now that his desires were satiated. In September, Anne was with child, and Henry was confident, from his consultations with the astrologers, that she would give birth to a prince; but on the 7th of that month, to his great chagrin, she became the mother to a princess. Yet this girl, so despised, became a greater monarch than her sire—for it was Elizabeth. By act of Parliament, the child was made heir to the crown, Mary, the daughter of Katharine, thus being bastardized. The Pope annulled the new marriage, and threatened to excommunicate Henry; but that monarch already had declared himself the head of the Church in his kingdom, and the breach thus opened between him and the Pope grew daily larger; the principles of the Reformation spread rapidly among the people, and the new doctrines were openly preached. Among those who refused to acknowledge Henry's supremacy in religious matters, was Sir Thomas More. He was, next to Wolsey, perhaps the most illustrious man of the age, and was far

purer and holier in his life than that prelate. No
one of his enemies ever spoke a word against the
beautiful character which he had always borne.
He had been lord chancellor, but resigned his
trust. He was now old and gray-haired, and was
worn out with faithful service to his country and
king. He was arrested and thrown into the
Tower. In vain did the cruel king endeavor to
get him to agree to his right to supremacy in the
Church—the conscientious old man would not do
that to save his life To his persecutors he replied :

"I am the king's true, faithful subject, and
daily beadsman. I pray for his highness, and all
his, and all the realm. I do nothing harm; I
say no harm; I think none harm; and wish
everybody good : and if this be not enough to
keep a man alive, in good faith I long not to live.
I am dying already ; and since I came here have
been divers times in the case that I thought to
die within one hour. And I thank our Lord, I
never was sorry for it, but rather sorry when I
saw the pang past; and therefore my poor body
is at the king's pleasure. Would to God my
death might do him good."

Anne was, without doubt, the one who persuaded Henry to the murder of this godly man. When More's daughter Margaret came to him in his prison, he asked :

"How is Queen Anne?"

"In faith, father, never better," she replied; "there is nothing else in the court but dancing and sporting."

"Never better!" said the old man; "Alas! Meg, alas! it pitieth me to think into what misery, poor soul, she will shortly come. These dances of hers will prove such dances, that she will spurn our heads off like foot-balls, but it will not be long before her head will dance the like dance!"

This was a remarkable prediction, and how true it proved, all readers of history know. After a year's imprisonment, More was brought to trial for high treason. He was pale and emaciated, yet made a most eloquent defence, declaring that he had never opposed the king's will, and in the matter of his religious supremacy had simply kept silence. But he was a doomed man, and sentence was pronounced against him. Upon his return to the Tower, his daughter Margaret forced her way to him, and clasping her arms around his neck, wept like a child. He bade her

a last farewell amid the sobs of the spectators.
When he approached the scaffold for execution,
he was calm as the pure sky over his head. His
wit did not forsake him to the last, for he said,
when told that the king had mercifully com-
muted his sentence of being quartered, to simple
decapitation :

" God preserve all my friends from such royal
favors !"

When the news came to Henry of his death,
he was engaged in some sport with Anne. He
stopt quickly, and with a gloomy frown, said,
" Thou art the cause of this man's death ;" and
leaving the room, he retired to his own apartment in great agitation.

The news of More's downfall spread a gloom
over the whole of Europe. Said the Emperor
Charles, " We would rather have lost the
fairest city in our dominions than such a counsellor."

The queen now began to manifest a change
of character. The celebrated Latimer had it is
said great influence over her conduct, he hourly
pointing out to her the many faults in her character. It may be too that she began to anticipate
a change in the king's affections. About this

time Katharine expired, and Anne felt herself to
be without a rival.

But not long after she became aware that the
only rival which she ever need fear had for
months been exceedingly intimate with the king.
In the beautiful and artful Jane Seymour, she
possessed indeed a rival whom she had just occasion to fear, for Jane was to be the cause of
her downfall.   It is said that upon Anne's entering the king's room one day unexpectedly, she
saw Jane Seymour seated upon the king's knee,
receiving his caresses with the utmost composure.
If a stroke of lightning had laid her royal husband dead at her feet, she could not have been
more shocked, and she gave way to violent anger.   The king fearing that his hopes of an heir
would be cut short, tried to calm her, but in
vain, and on January 29th, she gave birth to a
dead son. Henry was beside himself with passion
at the result, and stalked into her chamber, and
taxed her with imprudence.   She courageously,
but very imprudently laid the blame upon "that
wench Jane Seymour." Very slowly she revived
in health, but never in spirits.   Finding it impossible to send away her rival from court, she
chose to spend the most of her time in the quiet

shades of Greenwich Park. While there she must have thought remorsefully upon the fate of poor Katharine of Arragon, and of others whose necks she had brought to the block. She was very sad, perceiving that her influence over the king was at an end. One day while walking upon the banks of the Thames, she met Sir William Kingston, lieutenant of the Tower, who informed her that she was arrested on a charge of adultery. She fell upon her knees in the greatest agony, crying, "O Lord, help me! as I am guiltless of that whereof I am charged." She asked, if she was to go to a dungeon—but the lieutenant replied, no; she should have the chamber which she occupied at her coronation. This cruel reference to her days of triumph quite overcame the poor queen. "O, where is my poor brother?" she exclaimed, and "O, my mother! thou wilt die of sorrow."

That Anne had been too free in her conduct with certain persons cannot be denied, but no one can believe her guilty of the frightful charge against her. It was trumped up by Henry merely to get rid of her, that he might marry Jane Seymour. Anne was surrounded with spies, and all her delirious ravings were reported against

4

her. The gentlemen with whom she was charged of committing adultery—five in number—were likewise placed in the Tower. Under the tortures of the rack one of them, an ignoble fellow, confessed the charge. His name was Mark Smeaton, and he was a poor musician; and the idea that the queen had ever been guilty of improper conduct with him is wholly preposterous. His confession was made while dying with tortures and in the hope of a pardon. From her apartment in the Tower, Anne wrote a most pathetic letter to Henry, but it only inflamed him the more against her. On the 10th of May, she was indicted of high treason together with the five persons charged with her of the ignominious crime. Four of them persisted in declaring the queen innocent, and still were convicted. Mark Smeaton to save his head and himself from further pain, confessed, put his name to the document, and then had his head cut off that he might make no after confessions or retractions. Strange and horrible as it may seem, the queen's own brother was one of the four persons charged with improper intimacy with Anne, his own wife, a wicked and bold woman, appearing as evidence against him.

It is hardly necessary to say that the queen was found guilty ; for whatever the blood-thirsty king determined he was sure to accomplish. She was condemned to be beheaded or burned, as the king pleased. Anne heard the sentence without a moan, a word, or a change of countenance, but in a few moments clasped her hands and raising her eyes to heaven, said : " Oh Father ! oh Creator ! thou who art the way, the life, and the truth, knowest whether I have deserved this death." Turning to the judges, she added a few words, and in a calm manner left the court. The spectators had not a doubt of her innocence, for no evidence was there against her.

Cranmer at this time pronounced her marriage null and void, and that it always had been so— thus bastardizing Elizabeth, who afterwards became so powerful. The ground of Cranmer's decision was that Anne previous to her marriage with Henry was engaged to Lord Percy. While awaiting her execution she seems at times to have been bereft of her senses. She asked the lieutenant of the Tower why the execution did not take place sooner, that the pain might be over. He replied that the pain could not be much it was so subtle, to which she replied, laughing heartily: "I hear the executioner is very good, and I have a little neck." She wrote some verses, of which the following is a sample:

> "Oh death rock me asleep,
>   Bring on my quiet rest,
> Let pass my very guiltless ghost,
>   Out of my careful breast.
> Ring out the doleful knell,
> Let its sound my death tell;
> For I must die,
> There is no remedy,
> For now I die!"

Henry chose that Anne should be beheaded, and sent to Calais for a French executioner of good repute. The crownless queen was informed of this circumstance. All strangers were driven from the Tower, Henry being well aware that the execution was an awful outrage upon justice or even common decency. To the last Anne asserted her entire innocence of the crimes imputed to her. Her message to the king will ever be remembered for its sarcastic bitterness: "Commend me to his majesty," said she, "and tell him he hath been ever constant in his career of advancing me; from a private gentlewoman he made me a marchioness, from a marchioness a queen, and now he hath left no higher degree of honor, he gives my innocency the crown of martyrdom."

Anne Boleyn was beheaded at twelve o'clock, the noon of the 19th day of May. She was dressed in black damask, with a large white cape round her neck, and on her head a velvet hood. Her eye was bright, and a flush was in her cheeks, and she looked, it is said, fearfully beautiful. Scattered about the scaffold were some of the poor woman's enemies, but upon seeing them, she simply remarked: " I am come here to die; not to accuse my enemies." She asked the lieutenant to wait the signal of death until she could speak a few words to those around her, after which with her own hands she took off her hat and collar and lay down to the block. Her last words were, " O Lord God, have pity on my soul." She refused to have her eyes bandaged, and, it is said, after her head was severed from the body, the eyes and lips were seen to move. Thus ended the life of this woman, who from an humble station rose to be Queen of England—but to mount still higher—to the scaffold.

The relation which the history of Katharine and Anne bears to the fortunes of Lady Jane Grey will in the course of our narrative become

very evident to the reader; it will not be amiss
to notice here that already King Henry by pro-
nouncing his marriage with Katharine incestuous,
of course, rendered the offspring, the Princess
Mary, illegitimate; and by the decision of Cranmer that the marriage with Anne Boleyn was
" *always*" null and void, in consequence of her engagement to Percy, of course the Princess Elizabeth was placed in the same unpleasant position.
At this time, therefore, provided Henry's unjust
decisions were acquiesced in, the legitimate heir
to the English crown must have been found in
the person of Henry's sisters, or one of their
descendants.

The Reformation at this time was gaining
ground with considerable rapidity; not that
there was as yet a pure Protestantism in England, for such was not the case till Henry was
laid in his tomb; but the royal example of dis-
respect to the Pope was almost universally followed, and the people examined the religious
disputes for themselves. Parliament, at the in-
stigation of the king, suppressed all religious
houses having an income of less than £200 a
year; the lands, buildings, rents and all appur-
tenances falling into the king's exchequer, and

amounting to over a million of pounds sterling. Still later, the larger monasteries and the colleges likewise fell into the hands of Henry, who seemed never to be satisfied with his income.

The most momentous act of the century, perhaps, occurred about this time—the translation of the Holy Scriptures into the English tongue for the use of the people. Isolated copies of the Bible had for several years been very carefully circulated among the curious and learned, or those who favored the principles of the German reformers; but until now it was reckoned an offence for a layman to peruse so dangerous a book. It is said that Anne Boleyn, in Wolsey's time, possessed a copy which the prelate took away from the hands of a friend, to whom she had lent it, but which Anne coaxed Henry to oblige the cardinal to return to its owner. But now copies of the new translation were printed in Paris, and were attached by a chain to the reading-desk of every church in England, so that every man who knew how to read, could peruse the holy book.

CHAPTER III.

HAVING hastily sketched the history of Henry
VIII., previous to the times of Lady Jane Grey,
we now come to the event of her birth, which occurred in the year 1537. Henry, Marquis of
Dorset, the father of our heroine, we have before
remarked, was not a man whose character in all
its shades can command our admiration ; yet if
we may rely upon the statements of contemporary writers, he was possessed of remarkable personal courage, and was generally quite generous,
though he was troubled with fits of meanness, in
one of which he treated his mother disgracefully.
He was a man of some ambition, yet was much
fonder of retirement and the quiet joys to be

found in the bosom of his family, than of all the brilliant shows of the capital or court. He prided himself in keeping up the dignified magnificence of the ancient nobility upon his own estate, rather than in filling a conspicuous position at court. He resided. at the time Lady Jane was born, at his seat of Bradgate, in Leicestershire. It was situated on the borders of the celebrated Charnwood forest, about four miles from the town of Leicester. The building upon the estate was large and fine, and was constructed by Lady Jane's grandfather. It was built principally of brick, was square, with four turrets at each corner, and was a very commodious building. The park attached to it was extensive, being six miles in compass, and beautiful, and was surrounded by a high wall. On one side of the garden there ran a beautiful little stream. This stream was used to turn a mill on the family estate. The estate was of large extent, and was well wooded. Upon it there was a castle, called Groby Castle, situate about ten miles from Bradgate, which, but for the fact that it was in a ruinous condition, would undoubtedly have been the family resi. dence,—though it was originally constructed with an eye to defence from foes without, and conse-

c

quently was hardly suited to the age. The forest of Charnwood adjoined the family residence,
and was more than twenty miles in extent, and
was principally owned by Lady Jane's father,
which proves him to have been a man of large
possessions. It was called *the waste*, it being entirely destitute of population. The park of Bew-
manor also belonged to the Marquis of Dorset,
also the Burley park. By exchange of lands
with his sovereign, the marquis came into possession of an immense tract of land about Bradgate, upon which there resided but few people,
and those principally his own retainers. It cannot be uninteresting to the reader to contemplate
for a moment this scene of the childhood of Lady
Jane Grey. For here she spent all her early
years, not, as we know of, leaving it at all until
her seventh year. She was completely isolated
from the great world without. Her home was
one of the grandest in England, yet in the bosom
of a wilderness. It was in the heart of England,
and for miles around there was nothing but unin
habited fields and forests. There were thousands
of acres of grand old woods, and square miles of
open country, upon which there were waving
crops of grass and grain. The solitude would have

been painful to some, and yet to a girl of Lady Jane's disposition, was very pleasant. Upon the estate, indeed, in the family park, there was a fine hill, from which the view must have been exquisitely beautiful, for from it you can see into seven counties of England.

The customs of that age were, of course, far different from those of our time, yet there was enough of refinement and splendor to be entirely compatible with comfort. There were few books, no newspapers, and the amusements common to all classes were of the rougher sort, consisting principally of field sports. The apartments of the Bradgate residence were not fitted up with all the luxuriousness of the present age, yet there were in use at that time many of the articles of furniture which we consider indispensable. There were carpets, mirrors, easy chairs, handsomely carved tables and bureaus; there were clocks— but at this time, the *fork* was unknown at the table. The dinner was a meal around which a good deal of rigid etiquette was thrown, as at the present day among the English nobility. The gates of the castle were customarily closed, and the inhabitants, residents and guests, sat down to the table or tables according to rank and position.

The dinner generally consisted of various kinds
of meat, beef, mutton, and venison; there was
usually also a good supply of fruits, native and
foreign, as well as wine of several kinds. The
manners of the age were undoubtedly coarser
than those of our own, but there was a gorgeous-
ness in the housekeeping of the leading families
of the kingdom rarely seen now. The number
of retainers connected with some of the houses
of the old noblemen was large enough to consti-
tute a respectably sized village of the present
day.

But it is time for us to return to Lady Jane.
Little is known respecting her earliest years, but
the fact that she resided at Bradgate. She was
baptized with a good deal of ceremony at the
little church of Bradgate, the whole family without doubt being present. The Rev. Mr. Harding
was at that time the family chaplain, and baptized Jane at the font which stood in the middle
of the church, with a canopy hung over it. This
same Harding became a Protestant, and then re
canted and fell back into the Romish Church.
The family of the Marquis of Dorset was now
often at court, but Lady Jane was too young to
accompany them, and she was closely attached

to her studies. At a very early age her parents saw that she possessed an uncommon desire for knowledge as well as a remarkable capacity for it, and having no sons, they gave her every opportunity for storing her young mind with learning. Lady Jane was exceedingly fortunate in possessing the acquaintance of Roger Ascham, whose family resided not far from Bradgate. He was for years the preceptor of Lady Elizabeth, and taught Lady Jane the art of writing, and from him she gained a beautiful hand, he being an excellent chirographer. Lady Jane's preceptor was John Aylmer, afterwards Bishop of London, a man of excellent parts, and devoted to the Protestant religion. It is said, however, that Lady Jane received her earliest impressions in favor of Protestantism from Harding, who became afterwards an apostate. She rapidly stored her mind with knowledge, becoming a proficient in Latin, Greek, Chaldaic, Arabic, French and Italian. She wrote beautifully, and was skilful in instrumental music. She also studied philosophy, could read Plato in the original Greek with ease, and was delighted with Demosthenes. Under the guidance. of Aylmer she became a devoted child of God, being much fonder of her bible

and of gaining religious knowledge than of pursuing her study of the sciences and languages.
She was not, as some may imagine, a blue-stocking, for she was pleasant and attractive in her
manners and conversation.   That she was precocious cannot be denied, but there was nothing
unpleasant in her advanced condition of intellect.
Her voice was low and sweet, and she could sing
very beautifully.   That she owed her purity of
life to the piety which was a conspicuous trait
in her character, we have no doubt, for it was
her subsequent fortune to reside long at a court
which was anything but virtuous, and she was
for years surrounded by unprincipled men and
women, but not one of her enemies ever whispered
a word against the exquisite loveliness and
chasteness of her character.

The Marquis and Marchioness of Dorset treated
her with considerable severity, yet she was allowed to cultivate the acquaintance of certain
visitors of the family, and the one for whom she
seemed to have a special affection was the dowager Lady Latimer, who afterwards became Queen
of England, and still later, wife of Lord Seymour
of Sudley, lord admiral of the kingdom.

When only seven years old Lady Jane was in

the habit of accompanying her parents to court,
and, it is said, that at this age she was much admired for her beauty, her accomplishments, and
her gentleness. She here saw the Brandons with
whom she was connected, her mother being the
daughter of the Duke of Suffolk, who died in
1545. When Lady Jane was nine years old she
filled some office at court in the chamber of
Queen Katharine Parr, and as her career henceforth is intimately connected with the great men
and women of the age, it will be necessary for
us to recur to the general history of those times.

The very morning after the day on which
Anne Boleyn, was beheaded Henry VIII. married Jane Seymour. He was, it is said, attired
for the chase when the signal gun from the Tower
announced to him that Anne was beheaded. He
started up with joy, exclaiming, "Ha! ha!—the
deed is done! Uncouple the hounds and away!"
Jane Seymour was the oldest daughter of Sir
John Seymour of Wiltshire, and had seven
brothers and sisters. Her brother Edward afterward became Protector, and another brother,
Thomas, was Lord Admiral during the reign of
Edward VI. Jane is represented by all historians as being very beautiful, but the pictures of

her are by no means flattering, for they represent
her to be coarse and almost entirely devoid of
beauty. She certainly was devoid of all gentleness and goodness, or she would not have consented to wed Henry the day after his former
wife was beheaded. The historians may call her
beautiful, discreet and wise, but she certainly
was not good and virtuous: if she had been, her
heart would have been with the murdered Anne
instead of being filled with joy at her marriage.
In the course of English history there is no transaction which bears a more hideous aspect than
that of the king's sudden marriage with Jane
Seymour, almost before the heart of his former
wife was cold, and it will ever be remembered to
the disgrace of Jane that she willingly consented
to the marriage. In the month of June Henry
caused Parliament to pass a new act of succession, entailing the crown upon such issue as he
might have by Jane Seymour, and Lady Mary
about this time purchased peace with her father
by signing her name to a paper which declared
herself to be by birth illegitimate, her mother's
marriage with Henry being incestuous. Of this
deed of humiliation we shall say more in the
proper place.

On the 12th of October, Jane gave birth to
Prince Edward, and, after lingering in extreme
pain and sickness for nearly a fortnight, expired.
One cause of her death was the ceremony and
pomp which were thrown about the baptism of
the infant heir to the crown, and the king did
not treat her with the gentleness which any wife
in her situation should receive. When apprized
of her death he did indeed manifest some sorrow
but it was slight, and he very soon forgot it in
the pleasure of having a son and heir. In 1538,
the king contemplated marriage with Anne of
Cleves. Her portrait had been sent to Henry
through ambassadors, and principally through
the influence of Cromwell, a marriage was agreed
upon. Anne set out for England, and landed at
Deal, on the 27th of December. She rested at
Dover Castle until Monday. Henry was so
anxious to see her that he could not contain himself, and went in great haste to meet her. But
when he saw her he was much disappointed, and
Anne was also disappointed in him. He was
full of anger at Cromwell, who came near losing
his life at once. The king abused him ferocious-
ly for marrying him " to a great Flanders mare,"
and demanded that he should instantly devise

some means to break off the marriage. The poor
minister was in a sad predicament, and religious
perplexities, added to his present troubles, hastened his destruction.

Henry finding it impossible to evade the marriage, at last consented that the usual ceremonies
should take place, and accordingly with great
splendor they were married on the fifth of January. A few months after, the king saw the pretty Katharine Howard, and was the more dissatisfied with his condition. At last he determined
upon a divorce, and a convocation of the clergy
was called, which body, without a dissenting
voice, pronounced his marriage with Anne null
and void. The grounds for the divorce were,
that she had been previously contracted to the
Prince of Lorraine, and that the king did not
love her, never had loved her, and that there
were no hopes of issue by her. In a few weeks
Henry was again married—and this time to
Katharine Howard. Her history is one of so
much tragical interest, that we will recapitulate
the prominent events in her singular career.
She was the daughter of Lord Edmund Howard,
and had the great misfortune to lose her mother
at an early age—the greatest misfortune indeed

which could have befallen the poor girl. Lord
Howard left the motherless Katharine in the
care of his step-mother, the dowager-duchess
of Norfolk. This lady was careless of her charge,
and even went so far as to allow her to asso-
ciate with vile and depraved women in her
extreme youth, and Katharine became so cor-
rupted, that at twelve years of age she was in
love with a low-born fellow, named Henry
Manox, and their in macy was carried to the
borders of criminality. She about this time
formed an acquaintance with Mary Lassells, an
artful and wicked woman, who was destined to
have a ruinous influence over her. The intrigue
with Manox was broken off; but still later, a
young gentleman, Francis Derham, a favorite
with the old duchess, fell in love with Katharine, and through the help of Mary Lassells, contrived to gain access to her and press his suit.
That Katharine loved him, there can be no
doubt, for they exchanged love-tokens. She was
neglected by her kinsfolk, and was so influenced
by the love of Derham, that she finally became
engaged to marry him. He asked permission to
call her "wife," and she replied that "she was
contented to have it so." If this were all that

appears against Katharine Howard in the pages
of history, we might accuse her of imprudence,
but could not impeach her integrity. But without the counsels of a mother, she was left to commit not merely improprieties, but crimes. Her
grandmother saw that she was locked in her bed-
chamber every night, as the chroniclers of that
age gravely inform us, but the keys were stolen
privily away, and Derham made nocturnal visits
to Katharine. " He would bring strawberries,
apples, wine, and other things to make cheer
with," afterwards confessed Katharine Howard.
At length the news came to the old duchess--it
could no longer be concealed that Katharine,
young and passionate, had been seduced by Derham, or that they had acted towards each other
as husband and wife, not scrupling at all at addressing each other by those terms of relationship. Derham was obliged to fly, and her words
to him proved that she loved him, for she said,
with the tears streaming down her cheeks, "Thou
wilt never live to say to me, 'Thou hast
swerved.'" Katharine now was placed under
the care of women of virtue and principle, and
the story of her imprudence, on account of her
extreme youth, was hushed up or forgotten, and

what is a little strange, as she became further developed in age and character, she became modest, maidenly, and really virtuous in her life. She came to court, and Henry soon loved her. She was possessed of considerable beauty, and was exquisitely graceful in her manners. She was small and slender, and Henry loved her for a time more passionately than he had ever before loved a woman. They were married, and the king caressed her, flattered her, and made great demonstrations of his affection for her. Upon her bracelet was the device: "*Non aultre volonté que le sienne*"—"No other will than his." But amid the intoxicating splendors and pleasures of her position, poor Katharine felt that a sword was suspended only by a hair over her neck During the first few months of her wedded life rumors of her old imprudence began to creep through the purlieus of the court. She must have been in an agony of torment all the while, and still forced to appear happy. At last Katharine sealed her fate, by appointing her old paramour, Derham, private secretary to herself. That she did it to seal his lips in reference to the early portion of her life, as a matter of policy, hoping thereby to save her reputation for honor—to save her life indeed, we entertain no doubt. She shortly after had a long private interview with her cousin, Thomas Culpepper, to whom at one time, before the king saw her, it was thought she would be married, and made him a present at his departure. The king, meanwhile, was so fond of Katharine that he omitted nothing which could give her pleasure. On the 31st day of October, a paper containing an account of Katharine's early misdemeanor, was put into the king's hands by Cranmer. Mary Lassells had revealed the dreadful truth—had most wickedly betrayed her old friend and mistress. Henry was surprised, and treated the whole matter at first as if it were not founded in truth. But he sent for Lassells, the brother of Mary, to whom she had related the sad story, and he was firm in his statement in reference to the unfortunate queen. Derham was arrested, and confessed that he had been engaged to Katharine, that they had lived together as man and wife, but also most solemnly declared that not the slightest familiarity had taken place between them, since her marriage with the king. When Henry heard the confession of Derham, he burst into tears. He loved Katharine as devotedly as it was possible for so

gross a being to love anybody. The queen went
into convulsions. She was placed under arrest,
and Henry retired to Oatlands, during her exami-
nation. There was no difficulty in proving a
precontract, which would have been sufficient
cause for a divorce, but not sufficient to warrant
the execution of the queen. Therefore the council determined on a charge of adultery with her
cousin, Thomas Culpepper. Both Derham and
Culpepper were arraigned for high treason, and
condemned to death. They made no confessions
which implicated the queen since her marriage,
though they were put to the torture. Parliament
passed an act of attainder against the queen, and
several others, among which was the Lady Rochford. Katharine was, however, by this time, for
she had lain in prison several months, weary of
life. She was penitent, and now looked forward
to the future—to another sphere of existence, for
comfort. She freely confessed that before her
marriage, when she was a young and thoughtless
girl, she had been guilty with Derham, but that
she had been a true wife and faithful to the king.
When her confessor told her to prepare for death,
she replied: "As to the act, my reverend lord,
for which I stand condemned, God and his holy

angels I take to witness upon my soul's salvation,
that I die guiltless, never having so abused my
sovereign's bed. What other sins and follies of
youth I have committed, I will not excuse; but
I am assured that for them God hath brought
this punishment upon me, and will, in his mercy,
remit them, for which, I pray you, pray with
me unto his Son and my Saviour Christ." She
refused to admit that she was engaged to Derham—there was therefore no way for severing
the marriage-tie between the king and herself,
except by her death. She was allowed only two
days to prepare for execution, after the bill of
attainder had become a law; but she did not
wish longer time. Upon the scaffold she was
meek, yet courageous, and perished in a right
queenly manner. In the opinion of many at that
time, she was innocent of the main charge against
her, and consequently she received much sympathy. But the age was corrupt, and the people
so accustomed to blood, that they were amused
by such tragedies.

CHAPTER IV.

KATHARINE PARR, the last wife of Henry VIII., was a woman of excellent understanding and true piety, and the first Protestant queen of England. Her history is so intimately connected with that of Lady Jane Grey, that she will figure somewhat prominently in our pages. She directed the studies of Lady Jane, and was ever to her a kind friend and adviser. She also directed the studies of Edward VI. and Queen Elizabeth, and from her those illustrious personages derived their love for learning.

Katharine Parr was the daughter of Sir Thos. Parr, and was married at an early age to Lord Borough, a widower with several adult children.

He lived but a short time after his marriage, and Katharine was left a widow, though she was but fifteen years of age. Before her twentieth year, she married again, and this time the widower, Lord Latimer. While the wife of Latimer, Katharine was often at court, and exercised quite an influence over Henry VIII. In 1543, or a year after Katharine Howard was executed, Lord Latimer expired, and Katharine Parr was left for the second time a widow. She was not only very learned, very good and pious, but she was very beautiful and possessed great wealth. She was connected with some of the first families of the kingdom also, and was considered a prize. Although governed by strictly religious principles, yet this charming widow was by no means insensible to the attractions of a brave, handsome man. She was sought in marriage by Sir Thomas Seymour, who was brother to Jane Seymour, and therefore uncle to Prince Edward.

He was a favorite with his brother-in-law, the king; was gay, handsome, and brave, given to splendor in dress, was a fine courtier, yet he fell in love with the modest, studious, retiring widow, and what is perhaps strange, Katharine recipro cated his affection. Beneath all her gentle piety

there was a spice of romance which lends addi-
tional beauty to her character. Seymour was an
anti-papist, and this suited Katharine, and perhaps first led her to feel an interest in him ; but
soon by his charms of person and manner, he
completely won her heart.   She had fully resolved upon marrying him, when alas! another
suitor demanded her hand—a suitor who was not
accustomed to brook a refusal. When the young
widow heard of Henry's intention, she was hor-
ror-struck, and even told him that "it were better to be his mistress than his wife," so certain
was any woman of death who should marry him.
She was afraid of the royal murderer, but she
also loved Seymour, and hated to give him up.
He, however, retired from the contest, and Katharine became Queen of England.   At this time,
Henry was enormously fat, and was full of disease, so that he could scarcely walk.   A more
disgusting object, probably, the whole kingdom
could not produce. His wife was beautiful, wise,
pious, and what was to the king a matter of great
importance, she was wonderfully skilful as a
nurse.   The Protestant party in England took
courage, for it was known that Katharine was
heartily the enemy of Catholicism, being in her

religious opinions on that subject far in advance
of her royal husband. She was, too, an accomplished scholar, yet knew passing well how to
merge the scholar into the wife. She could dis-
course most learnedly upon questions of science
or religion, but she could also nurse her husband,
care for her household, and train her step-chil-
dren to love learning and piety. One of her first
acts was to endeavor to reconcile Henry to his
children, Mary and Elizabeth. She taught these
princesses to translate passages from the Scriptures, and Elizabeth imbibed a love for the principles of the Reformation, which never afterward
decayed.

Shortly after her marriage, Katharine wrote
her celebrated book—"The Lamentations of a
Sinner." It is written eloquently, and was at
that time a fine specimen of composition. The
king showed to her in many ways that he at least
partially appreciated her devotion to him, for he
granted her any favors which she asked, and
thanked God he had so good a wife. He was
full of pains, so bloated with dropsy that he had
to move by machinery, and was troubled with
the most terrible of tempers—yet Katharine
soothed him, nursed him, and bore with all his

humors. She was so devoted that she would stand upon her knees for hours together, applying palliatives to his ulcerated leg. A man who would not have returned such faithfulness with kindness, must have been more than a monster. Yet all this while Seymour, her old lover, was at court, and Katharine was obliged to guard herself carefully against the appearance of evil.

About this time, Lady Jane Grey came to court. Katharine gave her a state-office in her bed-chamber, though she was but nine years old, and thus she was brought under her guidance. Lady Jane was at this time noted for her studious disposition and her learning—was a beautiful girl, and being treated somewhat harshly by her parents at home, was the more willing probably to leave it for the kind nurture of the queen. It is well that we have given the reader a picture of the dissolute manners of the time, to be seen even in the briefest sketch of Henry's wives, for without it he cannot fairly appreciate the almost divine loveliness of Lady Jane Grey's character. We shall hereafter in the course of our narrative see the youth of the Princess Elizabeth—we have already seen the conduct of many distinguished personages of that age, yet with any of these con-

trast the Lady Jane, and how exquisitely fair
and beautiful she appears! Amid all this corruption, this licentiousness, and popular dissipa-
tion which characterized both sexes, this fair girl
grew up as a lily rears its slender stem in a nox-
ious slough, and unfolds its snowy petals to the
sun. It is the more wonderful, when we remember that her own father was by no means a man
of the best principles or conduct, and many of
her relatives were wicked and unprincipled persons. Young and beautiful, a mere girl, she
came to court to be a witness of all the folly and
crime which was perpetrated there. But she
could not have fallen into better hands. The
queen guarded her very carefully, and instilled
into her mind principles of the strictest virtue.

Katharine was in the habit of disputing with
the king on matters of religion, in a way which
pleased him, but one day when he was unusually
out of humor, she ventured to remonstrate with
him against a proclamation forbidding the use of
a translation of the Scriptures. He was angry,
and Gardiner, who was a Catholic, who was
present, as soon as the queen left, took occasion
to speak against her majesty. His egotism was
touched by Gardiner's praise of his great knowl-

edge, and he was so wrought upon that he gave
Gardiner liberty to draw up articles against the
queen. Everything was carefully concealed from
Katharine, but one day Wriothesley dropt from
his bosom the bill of articles, and they were
picked up by an attendant of the queen, and immediately carried to her. When the noble, but
betrayed queen read the bill, she fell into convulsions, and her shrieks reached the king in his
chamber. His heart relented, and he was carried
to see her, which greatly revived her. She conducted herself with great skill, unlike her prede-
cessors who had fallen under the displeasure of
the king.

The following evening the queen was well
enough to visit the king in his bed-chamber. She
was attended by her sister, Lady Herbert, and
the youthful Lady Jane Grey, who was the king's
niece. Lady Jane carried the candles before the
queen. Henry received his wife with pleasant
words, but in a short time brought up the old
religious controversy; but Katharine with con-
summate wisdom replied, "that she was but a
woman, accompanied with all the imperfections
natural to the weakness of her sex; therefore in
all matters of doubt and difficulty, she must refer

herself to his majesty's better judgment, as to her
lord and head; for so God hath appointed you
as the supreme head of us all, and of you, next
unto God, will I ever learn."

"Not so, by St. Mary!" said Henry, "ye are
become a doctor, Kate, to instruct us, and not to
be instructed of us, as oftentime we have seen."

"Indeed," replied Katharine, "if your majesty
have so conceived, my meaning has been mistaken, for I have always held it preposterous for
a woman to instruct her lord; and if I have ever
presumed to differ with your highness on religion, it was partly to obtain information for my
own comfort regarding certain nice points on
which I stood in doubt, and sometimes because
I perceived that in talking you were better able
to pass away the pain and weariness of your
present infirmity."

"And is it so, sweetheart?" asked the king;
"then are we perfect friends." He kissed her
with affection, and bade her depart. Thus did
Katharine narrowly escape the scaffold. The
next day she and the king were airing themselves in the garden, the queen attended by our
heroine, Lady Jane Grey, and others, when
Wriothesley, the lord-chancellor, with forty of

the guard, approached to arrest her majesty. He knew nothing of the change in the king's mind, and the first intimation which he had was the terrible outburst of Henry, "Beast, fool, and knave, avaunt from my presence!"

The queen was moved to pity for the discomfited chancellor, and said "she would become a humble suitor for him, as she deemed his fault was occasioned by mistake."

"Ah! poor soul," said Henry, "thou little knowest, Kate, how evil he deserveth this grace at thy hands. On my word, sweetheart, he hath been to thee a very knave!"

There was now a reaction, and the king was profuse in his expressions of tenderness to Katharine. His attentions were occasionally coarse and disgusting. He would lay his ulcerated leg upon her lap, and sometimes before the whole court; yet she bore it all with a smiling face. But again the fickle monarch grew weary of Katharine, and it is said was preparing a fresh accusation against her, on the charge of heresy, when in the midst of his awful and unrepented crimes, there came a summons which he could not disobey. The physicians so dreaded his hideous temper, that they dared not tell him he was dying; the queen herself could not summon courage sufficient to execute so awful a task, but Sir Anthony Denny approached the royal bed and said, " All human aid is now vain, and it is meet for your majesty to review your past life, and seek for God's mercy through Christ!" Henry looked up sternly and said: " What judge hath sent you with this sentence upon me?" Denny replied, "Your physicians." When the physicians came with medicine, he said angrily, " After the judges have once passed sentence on a criminal, they have no more to do with him; therefore begone!" It was proposed that he confer with a divine, but he would see no one but Cranmer, saying that he would repose a little first. He slept an hour, and when he awoke was faint and alarmed, and he sent for Cranmer, but when he was come the king was speechless. He was consumed with thirst, and wished some white wine to drink, but being told that his last moment was come, he exclaimed, " All is lost!" and expired. Thus perished this terrible monarch, whose vices and temper were so hideous that the nation, corrupt as it was at this time, heard the news of his death with a feeling of relief and joy. To Katharine his death must have

been a happy event, for previously, her life had
been a most precarious thing, hanging upon the
fickle will of her lord.   Lady Jane Grey was a
witness to this dreadful scene at court, but soon
after retired to her father's seat, at Bradgate.

In his will, Henry provided that the children
which he might have by Katharine Parr, should
stand immediately after Prince Edward in the
order of succession, and next Mary, and failing
Mary and her issue, the Princess Elizabeth, provided in the case of both these princesses that
they married with the consent of the counsellors
appointed to Prince Edward.   Failing Elizabeth
and her issue, Lady Frances, the mother of Lady
Jane Grey, was to be heir to the crown, the
claim of Margaret, Queen Dowager of Scotland,
being entirely passed over.

Edward VI. came to the throne in the year
1547, being ten years of age.   Lady.Jane Grey
was born also just ten years before.   The king
was learned; when he was but eight years old,
he was in the habit of writing letters to his father
in Latin.   He was docile, kind-hearted, and having had tutors who were Protestants, was strong·
ly inclined to the principles of the Reformation.
Strype says, he "is the beautifullest creature that

liveth under the sun ; the wittiest, the most amiable, and the gentlest thing of all the world."

The Earl of Hertford, who was brother to Sir
Thomas Seymour, and uncle to the king, was appointed protector of the realm, and governor of
the king's person during his minority, and Sir
Thomas Seymour was made lord admiral and
Baron Seymour of Ludley. The Earl of Hertford was also made Duke of Somerset, and many
other high-sounding titles were added, and many
offices were given to him. He was, in fact, the
master of England, and his ambition was at last
gratified. He was, however, liked by the people, for he was generous and princely in his deportment. The two brothers, the protector and
the admiral, were exceedingly ambitious of
power, and did not regard each other affectionately.

The coronation of Edward VI. took place with
the usual pomp, the Marquis of Dorset assisting
in the ceremonies; but whether his daughter,
Lady Jane, was present or not, is not known.
though it is quite probable that she witnessed
the gorgeous pageant. Katharine Parr retired to
her house at Chelsea, on the bank of the Thames,
where Sir Thomas Seymour, her old lover, saw

her privately. He was still a man of great beauty, and brave, as well as cheering in his manners. Katharine was thirty-five years old, still handsome, and still dreaming over her old love for the gallant lord-admiral. She was also immensely wealthy, and as queen-dowager possessed a very high position in society, and the relation in which she stood to the young king, gave her every opportunity to influence his conduct. But Seymour was extremely ambitious, and it is said at one time, contemplated a marriage with the youthful Lady Jane, in the hope that eventually she might come to the throne; but at last he concluded it was the wisest thing for him to marry Katharine Parr. The queen-dowager seems to have given herself almost unasked to him, for she loved him truly and passionately. The following is a specimen of her correspondence with her lover:

" My Lord,—

" I send you my most humble and hearty commendations, being desirous to know how ye have done since I saw you. I pray you not to be offended with me, in that I send sooner to you than I said I would, for my promise was but once

in a fortnight. Howbeit the time is well abbre
viated, by what means I know not, except weeks
be shorter at Chelsea than in other places.

"My lord, your brother, hath deferred answer-
ing such requests as I made to him, till his coming hither, which he says shall be immediately
after the term. This is not the first promise I
have received of his coming, and yet unper-
formed. I think my lady hath taught him that
lesson; for it is her custom to promise many
comings to her friends, and to perform none. I
trust in greater matters she is more circumspect.

"And thus, my lord, I make an end, bidding
you most heartily farewell, wishing you the good
I would myself.—From Chelsea.

"P.S. I would not have you to think that this
mine honest good-will toward you, to proceed of
any sudden emotion of passion; for as truly as
God is God, my mind was fully bent, the other
time I was at liberty, to marry you before any
man I know. Howbeit, God withstood my will
therein most vehemently for a time, and through
his grace and goodness made that possible which
seemed to me most impossible; that was, made
me renounce utterly mine own will, and to follow
his will most willingly. It were long to write

all the process of this matter: if I live I shall declare it to you myself. I can say nothing, but as my Lady of Suffolk saith, 'God is a marvellous man.'

"By her that is yours to serve and obey during her life,

"KATHARINE, the Queen. K. P."

Seymour persuaded Katharine to consent to a private marriage with him, two or three months after Henry VIII.'s death. The marriage was private, to escape the opposition which was sure to arise from certain quarters against it. Everything was conducted with the utmost secrecy until after they had been married a month or more, when Katharine wrote an affectionate letter to the young king. Edward answered it kindly, telling her if there was anything which she wished him to do, he would do it willingly. He was asked to give his consent to the marriage, which he did with pleasure. But when the news came to the ear of the Duke of Somerset, he was exceedingly angry that his own brother should have stolen a march upon him, and he insisted upon Katharine's returning all the jewels which she possessed as queen-consort having, he said, forfeited her right to them by her marriage. Somerset's wife was a proud, imperious woman, and completely swayed the duke. She could not bear that the wife of her husband's brother, as queen-dowager, should take precedence of herself. Soon after the detention of the jewels by Somerset, Katharine wrote her husband a letter, from which we make the following extract, at which the reader can hardly fail to smile. It shows that the good Katharine was, after all, subject to passions like the rest of her sex:

"This shall be to advertise you, that my lord your brother, hath this afternoon made me a little warm. It was fortunate we were so much distant, for I suppose else I should have bitten him. What cause hath he to fear having such a wife? It is requisite for him continually to pray for a short despatch of that hell."

The sentence, "What hath he to fear," has allusion to the inordinate ambition of Somerset, who feared the advancing fortunes of his brother and in fact he had some reason to fear him, for like himself, he was very daring in his ambitious projects. It was proper that the executors of Henry VIII. should elect one of their number Governor to the young king, but it was illegal

for Somerset to assume the control of the kingdom, and overturn the will of the late monarch.

His designs were still more treasonable, and
the lord admiral laid his plans to overthrow
his brother, the protector. Somerset entertained
the idea of marrying the young king to his
daughter, the Lady Jane Seymour, and Admiral Seymour hoped to checkmate him by marrying the king to his young friend, Lady Jane
Grey. This idea, it is said, originated with
Katharine Parr. Somerset hoped to secure Lady
Jane Grey to be the wife of his son. But Seymour sent one of his confidential officers to
Bradgate, where Lady Jane was staying, and
proposed that she should come and reside with
Katharine and Lord Seymour, who would take
care that she was well married.

The Marquis of Dorset asked, "with whom
will he match her?" "I doubt not you shall
see him marry her to the king," replied the
officer.

Lady Jane since the death of Henry VIII.,
had been pursuing her studies amid the shades
of Bradgate, and was now quite willing to join
her dear old friend and teacher, the queen-
dowager. Her parents, who were somewhat

ambitious, were also willing that she should
go, hoping thereby to make her fortune in a
royal marriage. She therefore went to Han-
worth, in Middlesex, where Seymour and Katharine were now staying. It was a beautiful
place, a small royal seat; and here Lady Jane
pursued her studies with great success. The
Princess Elizabeth was her companion, and the
contrast between these two young women was
very striking. Both were proud of learning,
both loved the cause of Protestantism, and both
were young; but while Elizabeth conducted
herself very imprudently and immodestly, Jane
was pure, sweet, and modest as the severest
critic could wish. Elizabeth was now nearly
sixteen years of age. It is said that before
Seymour married Katharine he contemplated
a marriage with Elizabeth, and that nothing
but the death of Henry VIII. broke it up. A
month after the decease of the king, Seymour,
says one historian, proposed marriage with Elizabeth, but she replied, "that she had neither
the years nor the inclination to think of marriage, and that she would not have any one
imagine that such a subject had ever been
mentioned to her, at a time when she ought

to be wholly taken up in weeping for the
death of the king, her father, to whom she
owed so many obligations, and that she intended to devote at least two years to wearing
black for him, and mourning for his loss; and
that even after she should arrive at years of
discretion, she wishes to retain her liberty without entering into any matrimonial engagement."
Katharine went so far as to talk with the princess in reference to the unsuitableness of such
a match, and the idea was given up. Elizabeth was now the guest of her lover, and
from the day of her entrance Katharine saw
but little joy.   At first the queen seemed to
encourage the admiral in his playful attentions
to Elizabeth, but at last her jealousy was fully
aroused.   Seymour stood high in the good
graces of Mrs. Ashley, the Princess Elizabeth's
governess, and would come into the young lady's bed-chamber before she was up, would
"strike her on her back familiarly," and "try
to kiss her in bed," and one morning when
Katharine was with him, "tickled Lady Eliz-
beth in bed."   One day Katharine, who began
to suspect Seymour loved Elizabeth, came suddenly into her room, when she was thunder-

struck to see her sitting in Seymour's lap, with his arms around her. The poor queen was cut to the heart, for she loved her husband dearly. She was greatly offended with both, and not merely on account of her husband's injustice to her, but because of the irreparable injury he was inflicting upon the character of the young princess. Already rumors were afloat of an unpleasant nature, and were the admiral guilty of the ruin of Elizabeth, he would justly be regarded by the nation as a monster. Whenever Seymour was praised in Elizabeth's presence she always manifested pleasure, and whenever his name was mentioned she blushed. There can be no doubt but that she loved him, and as to her guilt at this time it is better to say nothing, as nothing is positively known. The queen acted very wisely, for she sent her quietly away, and endeavored to hush all rumors against the reputation of the imprudent, if not criminal princess. It is refreshing to turn from the history of Elizabeth's youth to that of Lady Jane, who was the best-loved friend of Katharine. At this time the queen-dowager, naving hopes of an heir, went to reside at Sudley Castle, in Gloucestershire, a fine old residence. Somewhat sad from her recent discoveries in reference to her husband's affections, the queen was yet sustained with the hope of presenting him with an heir, which she fondly trusted would recall his wandering heart to its proper home. She took the lovely Lady Jane with her, who, although so young in years, yet was so gentle and wise, so beautiful and good, that she was a most desirable companion for her.

On the 30th of August, 1548, Katharine gave birth to a daughter, much to the disappointment of both parents, who had hoped it would prove to be a male heir. But Seymour did not express any regret, but seemed to be overflowing with exquisite happiness at the thought of being a father. But the queen gave birth to her babe at the cost of her own life. The puerperal fever attacked her, and finally caused her death. Seymour treated her very affectionately, but amid her half-delirium she seemed to hate him and even to forget her babe.

It is supposed by some that Katharine suspected that she was poisoned, but it is a very improbable supposition. The charge of poisoning was an after-invention of Seymour's enemies to ruin him with the king. It is more probable that some of the queen's attendants repeated to her some of the court gossip in reference to Seymour's passion for Elizabeth. Certain it is that she made her will upon her death bed, in which she bequeathed all her possessions to her dear husband, "only wishing them to be a thousand times more in value than they were." Upon her sick bed it is true she seemed to be sorely troubled with something in reference to Seymour. She said that she was not well handled. "Why, sweetheart," said her husband, "I would do you no hurt." He tried to pacify her, and laid down by her side and spoke kind words of affection to her, but she answered sharply. But it was mainly the disease, for she said not a word about her babe, which was unnatural. Seven days after the birth of her child, this good wife and excellent woman expired. Although she expressed herself somewhat severely against her husband, yet before she died her thoughts were all upon him, and her heart, too, was his. To the very last she loved him, and loved him so well that she was anxious that he should have all her wealth, even forgetting the babe in whose veins ran her own blood!

Lady Jane Grey was in close attendance upon the queen during her illness, and saw her eyes closed in death. It must have been a sad stroke upon her young and tender heart, for Katharine had been to her a preceptor, a friend, and a mother, the kindest mother she had in the world, if we may believe the words of Roger Ascham, her tutor.

The funeral of the queen took place with great solemnity from Sudley Castle, and Lady Jane Grey was the chief mourner. We extract the following from " a breviate of the interment of the Lady Katharine Parr, queen-dowager," which is still preserved. It certifies that Lady Jane was present at the funeral, and acted as chief mourner in the procession.

" The order in proceeding to the chapel :

" First, two conductors in black, with black staves ; then gentlemen and esquires ; then knights ; then officers of the household, with their white staves ; then the gentlemen ushers ; then Somerset herald, in the tabard coat ; then the corpse, borne by six gentlemen in black gowns, with their hoods on their heads ; then eleven staff torches, borne on each side by yeomen round about the corpse, and at each corner a knight for

assistance (four) with their hoods on their heads;
then the Lady Jane (daughter to the Lord-Mar-
quis Dorset) chief mourner, her train borne up
by a young lady; then six other lady mourners,
two and two; then yeomen, three and three, in
rank; then all other following."

We cannot take our leave of Katharine Parr
without quoting the words of a writer who lived
in her time:

" She was endowed with a pregnant wittiness
joined with right wonderful grace of eloquence,
studiously diligent in acquiring knowledge as
well of human discipline as also of the holy
scriptures; of incomparable elasticity, which she
kept not only from all spot, but from all suspi-
cion, by avoiding all occasions of idleness, and
condemning vain pastimes."

The queen's chaplain wrote her epitaph in Latin.   The translation is as follows:

"In this new tomb the royal Katharine lies;
    Flower of her sex, renowned, great, and wise
    A wife, by every nuptial virtue known,
    A faithful partner once to Henry's throne.
    To Seymour next her plighted hand she yields—
    Seymour, who Neptune's trident justly wields;
    From him a beauteous daughter bless'd her arms,
    An infant copy of her parent's charms.
    When now seven days this infant flower had bloomed,
    Heaven in its wrath the mother's soul resumed."

Of all the queens who were the consorts of Henry VIII., Katharine was the only one whose character for piety and wisdom is all that one could wish. Her influence over Lady Jane Grey was very great, and to her guidance we may ascribe much of Lady Jane's purity and nobleness of life.

7

CHAPTER V.

THE death of Katharine Parr was a terrible
shock to Lord Seymour; so keenly did he feel
it, so overwhelmed was he with the affliction,
that he resolved at once upon dismissing his
household, and giving up the splendor which
surrounded his housekeeping at Sudley Castle.
His plans were all broken up by Katharine's
death, and he scarcely knew how to proceed.
He, however, shortly reconsidered his decision,
and wrote to Lady Jane's father, earnestly re-
questing that she might remain at his house.
The following is a copy of the letter.

" My lord,

" After my most hearty commend unto your

lordship, whereby my last letter unto the same
written in a time when partly with the queen's
highness' death I was so annoyed that I had
small regard either to myself or my doings; and
partly then thinking that my great loss must
presently have constrained me to have broken
up and dissolved my whole house, I offered unto
your lordship to send my Lady Jane unto you,
whensoever you would send for her, as to him
whom I thought would be most tender to her.
Forasmuch, as being since both better advised
of myself, and having more deeply digested
whereunto my power would extend, I find that
indeed with God's help, I shall right well be
able to continue my house together without di-
minishing any great part thereof. And therefore, putting my whole affiance and trust in God,
have begun anew to establish my household,
where shall remain not only the gentlewomen of
the queen's highness' privy chamber, but also the
maids which waited at large, and other women
being about her grace in her life-time, with a
hundred and twenty gentlemen and yeomen,
continually abiding in house together; saving
that now presently certain of the maids and gentlemen have desired to have leisure for a month

to see their friends, and then immediately return hither again. And therefore, doubting lest your lordship might think any unkindness that I should by my said letters take occasion to rid me of your daughter so soon after the queen's death; for the proof both of my hearty affection towards you, and good will towards her, I mind now to keep her, until I next speak with your lordship; which should have been within these three or four days, if it had not been that I must repair unto the court, as well to help certain of the queen's poor servants, with some of the things now fallen by her death, as also for my own affairs; unless I shall be advertised from your lordship of your express mind to the contrary. My lady, my mother, shall and will, I doubt not, be as dear unto her, as though she were her own daughter, and for my own part, I shall continue her half-father and more, and all that are in my house shall be as diligent about her as yourself would wish accordingly.

" THOMAS SEYMOUR."

But the marquis seems not to have been willing that Lady Jane should remain, for two days after he wrote as follows to Seymour :—

" My lord,

" My most hearty commendations unto your good lordship not forgotten. When it hath pleased you by your most gentle letters to offer me the abode of my daughter at your lordship's house, I do as well acknowledge your most friendly affection towards me and her herein, as also render unto you most deserved thanks for the same. Nevertheless, considering the state of my daughter and her tender years, wherein she shall hardly rule herself as yet without a guide, lest she should for lack of a bridle take too much heed, and conceive such opinion of herself that all good behavior as she heretofore hath learned, by the queen's and your most wholesome instructions, should either altogether be quenched in her, or, at the least, much diminished, I shall in most hearty wise require your lordship to commit her to the governance of her mother, by whom for the fear and duty she oweth her, she shall most easily be ruled and framed towards virtue, which I wish above all things to be most plentiful in her; and although your lordship's good mind concerning her honest and godly ed-ucation is so great, that mine can be no more, yet weighing that you be destitute of such one

as should correct her as a mistress, and admon-
ish her as a mother, I persuade myself that you
will think the eye and oversight of.my wife
shall be in this respect most necessary.   My
meaning herein is not to withdraw any part
of my promise to you for her bestowing, for I
assure your lordship, I intend, God willing, to
use your discreet advice and consent in that behalf, and no less than mine own ; only I seek in
these her young years wherein she now standeth, either to make or mar (as the common saying is) the addressing of her mind to humility,
soberness, and obedience.   Wherefore, looking
upon that fatherly affection which you bear her,
my trust is that your lordship, weighing the
premises, will be content to charge her mother
with her, whose waking eye in respecting her
demeanor shall be, I hope, no less than you, a
friend, and I as a father, would wish.   And
thus wishing your lordship a perfect riddance
of all unquietness and grief of mind, I leave
any further to trouble your lordship.

   "From my house at Brodegate, the 19th of
September.   Your lordship's to the truly my
power.   HENRY DORSETT.

   "To my very good Lord Admiral: give this."

Lady Jane's mother also wrote to Seymour as follows :

" Although, good brother, I might be well encouraged to minister such counsel unto you as I have in store, for that it hath pleased you not only so to take in worthy that 'I wrote in my Lady of Suffolk's letter, but also to require me to have in readiness such good advices as I shall think convenient against our next meeting, yet considering how unable I am to do that hereto belongeth, I had rather leave with that praise I have gotten at your hand, than by seeking more to lose that I have already won. And whereas of a friendly and brotherly good will you wish to have my daughter Jane still continuing in your house, I give you most hearty thanks for your gentle offer, trusting, nevertheless, that, for the good opinion you have in your sister, you will be content to charge her with her, who promiseth you not only to be ready at all times to account for the ordering of your dear niece, but also to use your counsel and advice on the bestowing of her whensoever it shall happen. Wherefore, my good brother, my request shall hat I may have the oversight of her with your good will, and thereby I shall have good occasion to think that you do trust me in such wise, as is convenient that a sister to be trusted of so loving a brother.   And thus, my most hearty commendations not omitted, I wish the whole deliverance of your grief, and continuance of your lordship's health.

From Bradgate, 19th of this September.

Your loving sister and assured friend,

"FRANCES DORSETT."

Lady Jane was grand niece of Henry VIII., and, therefore, grand niece to Katharine Parr, but we can hardly conceive why Seymour should consider himself her uncle because he married Katharine, but Lady Dorset addresses him as a relation, a " good brother."

Seymour finally consented that Lady Jane should return to her father's house, and sent his steward with her, but a few weeks afterwards he became very desirous that she should return to his house.   He revived his old idea of marrying her to Edward VI., her second cousin.   Lady Jane was now nearly twelve years old, and very pretty.   She was staying in London with her parents at Dorset-house, near the Temple, and there Seymour visited Lord Dorset, and finally, by eulogizing upon the brilliant prospect in store for Jane, *i. e.*, her marriage with the king, he persuaded the marquis to again relinquish his lovely daughter to his care. He gave him five hundred pounds, as a part of two thousand pounds, which he had agreed to lend him, and refused any bond, saying that Lady Jane should be the pledge.

Seymour's ambition was towering, and long before this he had endeavored to win the young king over to himself. Indeed, he was partially successful, for Edward seemed to regard him with more affection than his brother the lord protector. He gave Edward money, made him various presents, and endeavored in every possible secret manner to get the king into his own hands. At last, he induced him to write a letter advising that he be appointed in the place of Somerset to the office of lord protector. This brought Somerset, who was absent in Scotland, at once back to court, and steps were at once taken to induce Seymour to relinquish his imprudent and ambitious project. He paid no attention, however, to any remonstrances which were addressed to him on the subject, until the council passed a resolution that he be sent to the

e

Tower, when he hastened to his brother and sought a reconciliation, which took place. He was contented but for a short time, his spirit being a restless one, and impelling him forward to his fate. Somerset wished to marry his son Lord Hertford to Lady Jane Grey, but Seymour wished her to marry the king, to defeat his brother's project. Hertford afterwards married Lady Jane's younger sister. Somerset hoped to marry the king to his own daughter, and, therefore, was deadly opposed to Seymour's plan of raising Lady Jane to the throne.

The lord admiral said publicly of Lady Jane Grey, that "she was as handsome a lady as any in England?" It is evident that the king was well affected towards Lady Jane, and the Protestant party were not at all averse to the admiral's project. She had been very carefully educated under the tutelage of Roger Ascham and Queen Katharine Parr, and the latter person always had in view her prospects for a royal position in her subsequent career. But the protector's influence was too great for any such plan to succeed, and Seymour seems in a manner to have given it up, though Lady Jane remained at his house until his arrest for treason.

The Princess Elizabeth was now sixteen years old, and Admiral Seymour renewed his old idea of marrying her. He was twenty years older than Elizabeth, but he was yet handsome and graceful, and she loved him. She allowed her governess, upon the death of Katharine Parr, to write him a letter of condolence, and, in a short time, the rumor was abroad that he would marry her. But according to Henry VIII.'s will, she must not marry without the consent of the council, and this could not be obtained. If she should still persist in marrying Seymour, she forfeited her right of succession to the crown. This, of course, she could not make up her mind to do. She was herself too ambitious and too wise to make any such sacrifice. But there can be no doubt that she loved Seymour, and, in fact, that she never really and truly loved any other man during her brilliant career. It was her impassioned love for Seymour that led her into so many imprudences with him. By nature she was extremely cautious, but with him she seemed to forget all etiquette. She scrupled not to say that she would marry the admiral if the council consented. Somerset declared that "he would clap his brother into the Tower if he became a suitor for Elizabeth's hand," and the quarrel between them broke out afresh. This threat exasperated Seymour, and he plunged reckless-ly into the maddest intrigues against the lord protector. He resolved even as a last resort to seize upon the king's person ; and a confederate re-vealing his plans, Somerset caused his arrest. He was carried instantly to the Tower, and was now shut out from all hope. It would seem that he need not have feared for his life when his own brother was in reality the ruler of the kingdom, but Somerset was fully resolved upon sacrificing the life of Seymour, and thus rid himself of a powerful rival and enemy. The Parliament found a bill of attainder, and he was sentenced to be beheaded. Several of the Princess Eliza-beth's friends were arrested, and she herself had apartments in the Tower, and was looked upon in the light of a prisoner. She wrote a bold and eloquent letter to Somerset, in which she said, "Master Tyrwhit and others have told me there goeth rumors abroad which be greatly both against my honor and honesty, which above all other things I esteem, which be these, that I am in the Tower, and with child by my lord admiral. My lord, these are shameful slanders."

The princess was obliged to guard her very looks during the trial and execution of her lover, for she was herself in great danger from the suspicions which were aroused against her. Seymour seems to have abandoned himself to his fate from the moment of his imprisonment. He was probably so fully aware of the nature of his brother's ambition, and of the sacrifices which he would make to it, that he knew there was no hope of pardon. Upon the scaffold he protested that he had never committed any treason against the king or his country. Before his death he procured some ink, and plucking off an aglet from his dress, with the point of it he wrote a letter to Elizabeth. He perished sadly, without any religious confession; Latimer says, " dangerously, irksomely, horribly." When the Princess Elizabeth was told of his terrible end, she had the wisdom to conceal her sorrow, simply saying, " This day died a man without much wit, and with very little judgment."

The only heir of Seymour's was the poor babe which purchased its life by the death of its mother, Katharine Parr. Lady Jane Grey was godmother to the little orphan, but in the hands of its cruel uncle Somerset and his wife, it fared

worse than it would have done at the hands of a
pirate.   It should have inherited wealth, but
everything was grasped by a strong arm away
from her.   At one time she was in charge of the
Duchess of Suffolk, at another, of the Marquis of
Northampton, but, in every case, she was cheated
and despoiled of her rights.   Though the daughter of a Queen of England, she had no home, nor
place where to lay her head.   She survived until
the age of thirteen, when she joined her sainted
mother in a sphere where cruelty and injustice
cannot exist.

We cannot contemplate the execution of Seymour without a feeling of horror.   Undoubtedly,
he acted with the rashest imprudence, and, in a
manner, may be said to have induced his fate,
by his wretched conduct, but there is something
terrible in his death, caused, as it was, by his
own brother.   The heart of Somerset must have
been made of stone, or he could not have seen
his nearest relative, his own brother, upon the
scaffold without a pang of sorrow.   But he seems
not to have exhibited the slightest feeling upon
the subject.   His only desire was to secure his
dissevered head—and, when his object was accomplished, he was happy again.   This is the

great stain upon his life. He was generally popular with the people, and they mourned him
when, still later, he met the same dreadful fate
which he had passed upon Seymour, but some
there were who must have remembered the
murder of his brother, and have felt that the
hand of Providence was plainly to be seen in his
own execution.

When Seymour was arrested, Lady Jane Grey
returned to her father's, at Bradgate, where she
continued her studies. In the year 1550 the
Marquis of Dorset was appointed itinerant justice of the king's forests, and remained principally at his seat in Leicestershire. In the month
of August the whole family, with many guests,
were assembled there. During this month the
good Roger Ascham, being appointed to a di-
plomatic mission in Germany, made a visit to
Bradgate to see his beautiful scholar, Lady Jane
He says : —

"Before I went into Germany I came into
Brodegate, in Leicestershire, to take my leave of
that noble lady, Jane Grey, to whom I was exceedingly much beholden. Her parents, with all
the household, gentlemen and gentlewomen, were
hunting in the park. I found her in her chamber

reading Phaedon Platonis in Greek, and that with as much delight as some gentlemen would read a merry tale in Bocace. After salutation and duty done, with some other talk I asked her why she would lose such pastime in the park; smiling she answered me: 'I wis all their sport in the park is but a shadow to that pleasure I find in Plato; alas, good folk, they never felt what true pleasure meant.' 'And how came you, madam,' quoth I, 'to this deep knowledge of pleasure, and what did chiefly allure you unto it, seeing not many women, but few men, have attained thereto?' 'I will tell you,' quote she, 'and tell you a truth, which perchance ye will marvel at. One of the greatest benefits that ever God gave me is that he sent me so sharp and severe parents, and so gentle a schoolmaster. For when I am in the presence of either father or mother, whether I speak, keep silence, sit, stand or go, eat, drink, be merry or sad, be sewing, playing, dancing, or doing any thing else, I must do it, as it were in such weight, measure, and number, even so perfectly as God made the world, or else I am so sharply taunted, so cruelly threatened, yea presently sometimes with pinches, nips, and bobs, and

other ways which I will not name for the honor
I bear them, so without measure misordered, that
I think myself in hell till the time come that
I must go to Mr. Elmer, who teacheth me so
gently, so pleasantly, with such fair allurements
to learning, that I think all the time nothing
whilst I am with him. And when I am called
from him I fall a weeping, because whatsoever
I do else but learning, is full of grief, trouble,
fear, and whole misliking unto me. And thus
my book hath been so much my pleasure, and
bringeth daily to me more pleasure and more,
that in respect of it, all other pleasures in
very deed be but trifles and troubles unto me!'
I remember this talk gladly, both because it is
so worthy of memory, and because, also, it was
the last talk that ever I had, and the last time
that ever I saw that noble and worthy lady."

The reader must remember that in Lady
Jane's time it was customary to correct children and even grown up young ladies very
harshly. But the Marquis of Dorset was a
severe man, selfish, avaricious, and formed of
a temper anything but pleasant. Any man who
will mistreat his mother will mistreat a child,
and the marquis treated his mother shamefully

8

He seems to have been ready at all times to barter Lady Jane away without consulting her feelings, and it is a wonder how she was so gentle and lovely with such treatment as she received at home. Perhaps it was because she was so large a portion of her life absent from home, and under the guardianship of the gentle and good.

Early in the next year Roger Ascham wrote Lady Jane a letter, which is still preserved. The following is a copy:—

"In this my long peregrination, most illustrious lady, I have travelled far; have visited the greatest cities; and have made the most diligent observations in my power upon the manners of nations, their institutions, laws, religion, and regulations; nevertheless, in such variety there is nothing that has raised in me greater admiration than what I found in regard to yourself during the last summer, to see one so young and lovely, even in the absence of her learned preceptor, in the noble hall of her family, at the very moment when all her friends and relatives were enjoying hunting and field sports---to find, I repeat, oh, all ye gods! so divine a maid diligently perusing the divine Phaedon of Plato;

in this more happy, it may be believed, than in her noble and royal lineage.

"Go on thus, oh best adorned virgin, to the honor of thy country, the delight of thy parents, thy own glory, the praise of thy preceptor, the comfort of thy relatives and acquaintances, and the admiration of all. Oh happy Elmer! to have such a scholar, and to be her preceptor. I congratulate both you who teach, and she who learns.

" These are the words of John Sturmius unto myself as my reward for teaching the most illus-trious Lady Elizabeth ; but to you two I can repeat them even with more truth ; to you two I concede this felicity, even though I should have to lament want of success where I had ex-pected to reap the sweetest fruits from my labor.

" 'But let me restrain the sharpness of my grief, which prudence makes it necessary I should conceal even to myself. This much I may say, that I have no fault to find with the Lady Elizabeth, whom I have always found the best of ladies, nor indeed with the Lady Mary ; but if ever I shall have the happiness to meet my friend Elmer, then shall I repose in his bosom my sorrows abundantly.'

"Two things I repeat to thee, my good Elmer—for I know that thou wilt see this letter—
that by your persuasion and entreaty the Lady
Jane Grey, as early as she can conveniently,
may write to me in Greek, which she has already promised to do. I have even written
lately to John Sturmius, mentioning this promise. Pray let your letter and hers fly together
to us. The distance is great, but John Hales
will take care that it shall reach me. If she
even were to write to Sturmius himself in
Greek, neither you nor she shall have cause
to repent your labor.

"The other request is, my good Elmer, that
you would exert yourself so that we might
conjointly preserve this mode of life amongst
us. How freely, how sweetly, and philosophi-
cally, then, should we live! Why should we,
my good Elmer, less enjoy all these good things,
which Cicero, at the conclusion of his third
book, De Finitus, describes as the only ration-
al mode of life? Nothing in any tongue, nothing in any times, in human memory, either
past or present, from which something may not
be drawn to sweeten life!

"As to the news here, most illustrious lady,

I know not what to write. That which is written of stupid things, must itself be stupid; and,
as Cicero complained of his own times, there is
little to amuse, or that can be embellished. Besides, at present all places and persons are occupied with rumors of wars and commotions,
which for the most part are either mere fabrica-
tions, or founded upon no authority; so that
anything respecting continental politics would
neither be interesting nor useful to you.

" The general council of Trent is to sit on the
first of May: Cardinal Pole, it is asserted, is to
be the president. Besides, there are tumults this
year in Africa; then preparations for a war
against the Turks: and then the great expec-
tations of the march of the emperor into Hun-
gary, of which, though no soldier, I shall, God
willing, be a companion. Why need I write to
you of the siege of Medgeburg, and how the
Duke of Mechlenburg has been taken; or of
that commotion which so universally at this
moment afflicts the miserable Saxony? To
write of all these things I have neither leisure
nor would it be safe; but on my return, which I
hope is not far distant, it shall be my great happiness to relate all these things to you in person.

"Thy kindness to me, oh most noble Jane Grey, was always most grateful to me when present with you; but it is ten times more so during this long absence. To your noble parents I wish length of happiness; to you a daily victory in letters and in virtue; to thy sister Katharine, that she may resemble thee; and to Elmer I wish every good that he may wish to Ascham.

"Further, dearest lady, if I were not afraid to load thee with the weight of my light salutations, I would ask thee, in my name to salute Elizabeth Astley, who, as well as her brother John, I believe to be of my best friends; and whom I believe to be like that brother in all integrity and sweetness of manners.

"Salute, I pray thee, my cousin Mary Laten, and my wife Alice, of whom I think oftener than I can now express. Salute, also, that worthy young man Garret, and John Haddon.

"Farewell, most noble lady in Christ.

"R. A.

"AUGUSTAE, 18th January, 1851."

It would be a singular sight, even in this enlightened age—that of a girl of fourteen years corresponding with the first scholars of

Europe, and in Greek! Ascham, Bullinger, and
Sturmius, all distinguished men, received her letters with the greatest pleasure, and answered
them as if it were a wonderful privilege. In the
following month of June, Lady Jane commenced
the study of the Hebrew language, and in the
same month wrote an epistle to the celebrated
Bullinger, at Zurich. Bullinger was imbued
with the principles of the reformation, and was
well known to the Dorset family. The letter
of Lady Jane is unaffected, the style pure, and
the sentiments religious. During a part of the
year 1551, Lady Jane resided in Cambridge,
though the greater portion seems to have been
spent at Bradgate. On the 11th of October her
father, the Marquis of Dorset, was raised to the
peerage. The title of the Suffolk family had
become extinct by the death of Henry and
Charles Brandon, and it was bestowed upon the
Marquis of Dorset, because his wife was sister
to the Suffolks. From this time, therefore, we
shall mention Lady Jane's parents by their new
titles—the Duke and Duchess of Suffolk.

The family now came to London, and Lady
Jane was presented at court. Mary of Lorraine,
the queen-dowager of Scotland, had just arrived

from France, and on the occasion of her visit
Lady Jane publicly took part in the ceremonies
in honor of the queen. The first interview
between the queen and King Edward took
place on the fourth of November, and Lady
Jane was a witness to the interesting scene.
The reception took place at Whitehall, and
the Duchess of Suffolk rode in the carriage
thither with Queen Mary, and her daughter,
Lady Jane Grey, followed in her train. That
day the royal couple dined alone together, and
Lady Jane, her mother, and many other distinguished ladies, retired to the queen's great chamber, where they all partook of a grand entertain-
ment. That night her majesty returned to her
apartments in the bishop's palace, but two days
afterwards further honors were conferred on
her. A long train of the nobility followed her
through Bishopsgate street as far as Shoreditch
church, and Lady Jane's mother, the Duchess of
Suffolk, was a very prominent personage in the
procession, adding much to its splendor.

On New Year's day, 1552, the Duchess of
Suffolk made Edward the king a present of a
purse knit of gold and silver, and containing
forty pounds sterling. The young monarch gave

her in return three gilt bowls with covers.
Edward often saw Lady Jane, and loved her,
but rather as a brother than as a suitor. It
was about this time that Lady Jane wrote a
second letter to Bullinger, the scholar and
reformer.

The health of Edward declining at this time,
it was proposed that he should travel over the
kingdom, in the hope of diverting his mind from
weighty matters which pressed upon him. Just
previous to his starting, the Princess Mary came
to court and had an interview with her half-
brother. The King started for Guildford the
latter part of June, and in July Lady Jane
Grey took occasion in the absence of the court
to pay a visit to the Princess Mary at Newhall.
The princess seems to have received her in a
cordial manner, though they did not agree upon
religious subjects. The following anecdote is recorded as having occurred during this visit. The
Princess Mary was at heart a Catholic, though
she made pretences of being, if not a Protestant,
at least very liberal in her religious belief. She
had a domestic chapel at Newhall, and one day
when Lady Jane Grey was walking through it
in company with Lady Wharton, the latter curt-

F

sied to the host on the altar. Lady Jane observed the act of reverence and asked,

" Is Lady Mary present in the chapel ?"

" No," replied Lady Wharton.

" Why, then, do you curtsey ?" asked Lady
Jane.

" I curtsey to Him that made me," replied
Lady Wharton.

" Nay," said Lady Jane," but did not the
baker make him ?"

This dialogue was repeated to the Princess
Mary, who was offended with Jane, and it is
said never afterwards loved her. We may be
sure of this fact, but we doubt if ever before
she entertained much affection for her lovely
cousin. She did at one time, to be sure, present her with a costly dress, yet Lady Jane
said, when the dress was sent to her,—

" Nay, it were a shame to follow my Lady
Mary, who leaveth God's word, and leave my
Lady Elizabeth, who followeth God's word."
The Princess Elizabeth for several years had
endeavored by a sober and severe life to expiate
her sad imprudencies with Lord Seymour. It
may have been that the dreadful fate of the
only man whom she truly loved made so deep

an impression upon her mind, that she was desirous of quitting the vanities of life. Several years before, Mary gave to Lady Jane a gold necklace set with pearls. Alas! the fair neck around which the golden gift was placed, was destined to be severed by the same hand which offered the splendid toy! It is quite evident that Lady Jane never looked upon Mary with much affection. Her conduct, indeed, had not been attractive, and her sympathies for Catholicism might have rendered her odious in the sight of the pious and enlightened Lady Jane.

The king continued absent on his journey, and Lady Jane Grey returned to her studies. The good Aylmer was her guide and instructor, and she was a most apt pupil. Not only was she thoroughly acquainted with the learned languages, but general science attracted her close attention. She was also deeply versed in theology, so much so that she was a match for almost any religious disputant.

CHAPTER VI.

THE Duke of Somerset, when he had sacri
ficed the life of his own brother to his ambition,
became still more desirous of enlarged power and
influence. A great commotion raged throughout England among the lower classes, on account of a pecuniary panic which was prevalent
in the country. The duke, hoping to add to
his popularity with the masses, took the side
of the people. The landholders in many instances had inclosed the commons, which the
poor people had been accustomed to graze their
cattle upon, or otherwise make use of, and the
protector somewhat rashly issued a proclamation insisting that all commons which had been
inclosed should at once be thrown open to the
public. But few obeyed this proclamation, and

the masses determined to rectify the evil by mob-law, and insurrections were common over the kingdom. The landed proprietors and the nobility, by this act of Somerset, were alienated from him, and resolved to affect the ruin of so bold and despotic a man. Though themselves guilty of usurpation of lands, they yet saw that the duke had assumed a power which he could not legally hold.

Religious revolts soon agitated the kingdom, which had their seat in the west, and also in Oxfordshire and Buckinghamshire. The people who revolted were principally of the laboring classes, and they generally revolted against the oppression of the wealthier classes rather than Protestantism, though in certain parts great dissatisfaction was felt at the religious state of the government. The protector had been unfortunate in his wars, in his statesmanship; had been personally extravagant, building himself a most costly palace at a time when the nation was almost bankrupt ; and a storm had now arisen which he could not withstand. In his war with Scotland he had been unsuccessful; in his conflict with France he had been defeated ; the old nobility had from the first hated him ; and now in a time of unprecedented depression in pecuniary matters, his extravagance was such as to disgust the nation. Conceited, vain, and ambitious, he caused himself to be styled " Duke of Somerset by the grace of God," after the most royal manner. At this time there was a man in England who had the acuteness to perceive that Somerset's fall was inevitable, and he determined to profit by it. He was a man of fearful ambition, who would not scruple at any act by which he might advance his fortunes; a man who knew passing well how to cajole and flatter, indeed how to control men, and yet he was by no means possessed of the highest talent, and had little personal courage. He was a renowned soldier, possessed no settled religious principles, but discovering how firm the young king was in his devotion to the Reformation, he became a Protestant.

This man, who exercised such a sad influence over the fortunes of Lady Jane Grey, was the Earl of Warwick, afterwards made Duke of Northumberland. He was born in 1502, and was in early life attached to Cardinal Wolsey. He achieved many victories by land and sea, and now, seeing plainly that Somerset was hated by

the nobility, and was losing his popularity with
the people, he began to play a bold game for
power.   He endeavored to win the affections of
the king, and, being one of the council, soon
came to be Somerset's only great rival.   But
Somerset was growing unpopular, his star was
setting in the west, while that of Warwick had
but just arisen. The latter part of the year 1549,
the enemies of Somerset were so bold in their
measures against him, that he became alarmed,
and surrounded himself with soldiers well
equipped for defence. He was at Hampton Court,
and the king was with him.   Somerset carried the
king to Windsor, while the council, animated by
Warwick, called upon the nobility throughout
the kingdom to come to their assistance.   Somerset first determined to defy his enemies, and,
by force, if necessary, retain possession of the
monarch, but he very soon wrote a letter to the
council, in which he stated, that provided they
intended no harm to the king, they would find
him, the protector, ready to agree to their re-
quirements.   They saw, at once, that Somerset
was at their feet.   Warwick had triumphed.
The council published a proclamation, in which
they stated clearly the misconduct of the protec-

tor, who, at last, wrote privately t nis great
enemy, Warwick, and begged of hin. to save
him, reminding him of their friendship in older
days.   On the 13th of October, Somerset was
placed under arrest, and the misdemeanors of
which he was guilty, were drawn up against him
in writing, and he was carried to the Tower.
Thus Warwick was left at the head of the government, and, of course, had constant access to
the king, whom he soon completely controlled.
In 1550, Somerset made a humble confession,
that he had been guilty of the misdemeanors
charged against him, on his knees before the
king, in the hope that he would be dealt mercifully with.   He was deprived of all his offices,
of all personal property, and of two thousand
pounds a year from the revenue of his lands.
He complained of the severity of this heavy fine,
but when the council replied harshly to him, he
confessed that it was just.   As a reward for his
abject humility, he was, on the sixth of February, released from the Tower.   He conducted
himself so humbly that he was again sworn in
member of the privy council.   The Earl of Warwick was made lord admiral, and great master
of the household.   An apparent reconciliation

took place between Warwick and Somerset; Lord Lisle, Warwick's eldest son, marrying Lady Anne, daughter of Somerset. But the late lord protector could not be content with his present humble position, and took secret measures for re- aining his old position. He conceived the idea of getting the king into his hands, and making a stand in the provinces. In October, Warwick was made Duke of Northumberland, and shortly after, the nation was shocked by the news that Somerset was again arrested, and, this time, on a charge of high treason. It was charged that he had intended to raise a revolt against the gov- ernment in conjunction with other noblemen, that he designed taking possession of the king; and to prove these charges, the confessions of one of his tools were taken as evidence. The trial took place on the first of December, the duke being brought from the Tower to Westminster, with the axe of the Tower carried before him. The trial was a most unfair one, yet fairer than the trial which Somerset had acceded to his own brother, Admiral Seymour. He denied the charge against him, though he confessed that he had, at one time, prepared to kill Northumber- land, but had afterwards given up the idea. The

f
9

charge of treason fell through, but he was found guilty of felony, and sentenced to be beheaded. He was carried back to the Tower, unaccompanied by the terrible axe, inasmuch as he had been acquitted of the charge of treason.

The execution took place on Friday, the 22d of January, and the king, in his journal, thus early makes a note of his uncle's death:

"The Duke of Somerset had his head cut off upon Tower-hill, between eight and nine o'clock in the morning."

Early in the morning, London was astir, for though the Duke of Somerset had been a proud, ambitious and extravagant man, yet the people could not entirely lose their old love for him, and now that his day of doom had come, their sympathies were deeply roused. The Lord-Mayor of London and the constables required that every household remain within doors until after ten o'clock, to prevent a gathering of the people, or an insurrection. Notwithstanding this order, by seven o'clock Tower-hill was covered by an immense multitude of people. The duke was perfectly calm, kneeling down, and repeating a few short prayers. After this, he rose, and walked to the east side of the scaffold, and spoke

to the people. He said that he had never by
word or deed offended against the king, and that
he did not repent at any of his doings while
lord protector. He certainly must have forgotten his base treatment of his brother Seymour,
or else he spoke hypocritically. While he was
speaking, a great noise was heard, and a man
was seen to ride swiftly towards the Tower. Immediately there rose a great cry of "A pardon!
a pardon! God save the king!" The duke informed the people that they were mistaken,
though, at first, it is likely that he himself had
faint hopes that the horseman might bear news
of a reprieve. He requested the multitude to be
quiet lest their tumult should disturb his calmness, which was so desirable at such an hour.
He then knelt down again, and prayed with
seeming fervency, the people watching him with
swelling hearts, and some with streaming faces.

He then stood up before them, and with a
clear, calm face bade the sheriffs farewell, then
the Lieutenant of the Tower, and all others on
the scaffold with him. He gave the executioner
some money, and then took off his gown, and
knelt down on the straw, untying his shirt-
strings, and turning his collar down from his

neck, that his head might be severed easily and quickly. When he laid his neck upon the block his cheeks grew red, but immediately a cap was put over his face. He repeated the name of Jesus slowly, and, at the third time, the axe descended, and he was instantly killed. Hundreds of the spectators rushed up and dipped their handkerchiefs in the blood, that they might keep them in memory of the beheaded duke. This proves pretty clearly that the people yet loved him; still they remembered how a few years before, he had sacrificed the life of his brother without the least hesitancy or apparent compunction of conscience. The fate of the duke, therefore, seemed to be a judgment of God, and whether or not he deserved his fate on account of treason to the state, or felony, it is pretty certain that he deserved it on account of his own criminality in other transactions. Several persons perished with the Duke of Somerset as his accomplices, and among them Sir Ralph Vane, who, well knowing that the Duke of Northumberland was at the bottom of their murder, said boldly, that as often as Northumberland laid his head on his pillow he would find it wet with their blood. Whether or not it was so, the

duke was destined to feel the retributive hand
of Providence a few years later.

Parliament met the day after the execution of
Somerset, and it was found that the members
could hardly be counted on as the hearty sup-
porters of the existing government.

The truth was, that the Duke of Northumberland by his execution of Somerset had outraged
the feelings of the nation, and they soon learned
to hate while they feared him. He met with
bold opposition in parliament, and out of it, and
if he now would, he might have learned a lesson
which would have saved his life. But his ambition was so towering, that opposition only
whetted his appetite for more power, and his
schemes grew still bolder and more magnificent.
He, at one time, purposed to marry his son, Lord
Guildford Dudley, to the daughter of the Earl of
Cumberland, and, it is said, the king planned
the match, and if so, it renders probable the
story, that he was himself attached to Lady Jane
Grey, and intended to make her his wife. But
Northumberland soon dropped this project for a
new vision opened upon his ambitious eyes.
The king, for some time, had been declining in
health, and was now so seriously ill as to alarm

the nation.   His constitution ever was delicate ·
in the spring of the previous year, he was attacked by the measles and small-pox, and being
ill for a long time, his frame was very much en-
feebled, and it seemed impossible for him to re-
gain even his accustomed robustness.   In the
spring of 1553, he caught a violent cold, which
was aggravated by injudicious treatment, and a
disease of the lungs was the consequence.   Some
declared that he was under the influence of slow
but subtle poisons, administered to him by
persons at court, but there is not the slightest
foundation for a belief in any such story.   Undoubtedly, that slow but terrible disease, the
consumption, was fastened upon the young, but
wise and pious king, and the Duke of Northumberland saw that he probably had not long to
live.   It was this state of things which aroused
the fiery ambition of his nature, and led him to
project schemes which were destined to prove the
ruin of not only himself, but of many others, among
whom, stands first and fairest, the gentle Lady
Jane Grey.   The duke saw that the young king
was warmly devoted to Protestantism, knew that
Edward was well aware of the Princess Mary's
half-concealed love for the Catholic religion, and

he trusted that he could persuade him to overturn the will of Henry VIII., and leave the
crown to Lady Jane Grey. It was a wild and
unrighteous project, which was probably entirely
concealed from the duke's best friends until
ripe for execution, and kept carefully away from
Lady Jane until after the death of the king.
Northumberland proposed that his son, Lord
Lord Guildford Dudley, should marry Lady
Jane, and thus he would be father to the Queen
of England, provided his plan should succeed.

CHAPTER VII

LADY JANE GREY.—DESCRIPTION OF HER PERSON.—HER LEARNING AND VIRTUES.—NORTHUMBERLAND'S PROJECTS.—IMAGINARY CONVERSATION BETWEEN ROGER ASCHAM AND LADY JANE.—HER MARRIAGE WITH LORD GUILDFORD DUDLEY.—EDWARD VI. A VICTIM TO NORTHUMBERLAND.—MAKES HIS WILL IN FAVOR OF LADY JANE GREY.—TROUBLES WITH THE COUNCIL.—INNOCENCE OF LADY JANE.

LADY JANE GREY was now sixteen years old, and, perhaps, one of the most beautiful women in England. Her beauty was of a style somewhat rare in that age. She was not commanding, imperious and passionately beautiful. Her beauty was surmounted by the most exquisite loveliness of character. She was gentle, kind and affectionate; though a learned scholar, she was no mere "blue-stocking." A painting of her at this time, which is still preserved, represents her as having a very fair, broad and beautiful brow, eyebrows of jet, a small and exquisite mouth, and a face on which sits the very spirit of meekness and subdued beauty. She wears a

very large head-dress, which almost entirely covers her hair from sight. A few locks are
seen upon the temple. Around her neck there
is a high collar or partlet, as it was called, standing upright, and very richly embroidered. The
neck and a slight glimpse of the bosom are to be
seen—in the latter, there is a beautiful bouquet
of flowers. Gowns at this time were generally
cut square in the neck, and were often splendidly
enriched by costly sleeves and a habit-shirt, the
collar of which standing upright was ingeniously
and handsomely embroidered.

A Holbein painting of Lady Jane represents
her without her partlet, her neck and bosom
almost bare, with the exception of necklaces and
jewels. Her hair in this painting is surmounted
by a low head-dress, and falls down upon the
back of her neck. In both pictures, the face is
very sweet and beautiful, and in the latter, there
is a pensiveness which would almost make one
suppose that, when it was taken, she anticipated,
by presentiment, her sorrowful fate.

Burton, an ancient writer, says of Lady Jane:
" That most admired Princess, Jane Grey, who
being but young, attained to such excellent learning, both in Hebrew, Greek, and Latin tongues,

and also in the study of divinity, by the instruction of Mr. Aylmer, as appeareth by her many writings, letters, etc., that as Mr. Fox saith of her, had her fortune been answerable to her bringing up, undoubtedly she might have been compared to the house of Vespasiaus, Lemproniaus, and Cornelia, mother of the Gracchi, in Rome; and, in these days, the chiefest men in the universities."

Fox says:

"She hath the innocency of childhood, the beauty of youth, the solidity of middle, the gravity of old age, and all at sixteen; the birth of a princess, the learning of a clerk, the life of a saint, yet the death of a malefactor for her parents' offences. I confess I never read of any canonized saint of her name; a thing whereof some papists are so scrupulous, that they count it an unclean and unhallowed thing to be of a name whereof never any saint was—but let this worthy lady pass for a saint; and let all great ladies which bear her name imitate her virtues; to whom I wish her inward holiness, but far more outward happiness."

Still another writer says:

"She had a perfection noble and holy, a

strength remarkable in one of her sex, a lady in all goodness so perfect that whosoever could gain but some part of her shadow, might have enough in latter days to boast, and rank themselves with the most virtuous."

Fuller says:

" No lady which led so many pious, lived so few pleasant days ; her soul was never out of the nonage of afflictions, till death made her of full years to inherit happiness ; so severe was her education. Whilst a child, her father's house was a house of correction ; nor did she write woman sooner than she did subscribe wife, and, in obedience to her parents, was unfortunately matched to the Lord Guildford Dudley, whose worse fault was that he was son to an ambitious father "

Sir Thomas Chaloner, in an elegy upon her death, commends her beauty, but much more her charming conversation. He says, she was well versed in eight languages ; had natural wit, and that much improved by art and study ; that she played instrumental music well ; wrote an excellent hand ; yet was mild, humble and modest, " and never showed an elated mind until she manifested it at her death." Lady Jane not only played on instruments, but had a very sweet voice, and sang beautifully, according to contemporary writers.

Bishop Latimer says :

" She was handsome, learned beyond imagination, of a most acute wit, and for prudence even at her age superior to her sex ; extremely pious ; devoted to the reformed faith ; and so far from aspiring to the honor, that she took the regalia with tears."

And Burnet says :

" With all her advantages of birth and parts, yet she was so humble, so gentle, and pious, that all people both admired and loved her, and none more than the youthful Edward."

The young king continued to grow worse, and the Duke of Northumberland resolved upon carrying out his daring projects in reference to the crown. The Parliament met in March of this year (1553), but sat only four weeks, leaving Northumberland in possession of the government. The monarch was in such ill health that his will was completely subjected to that of the duke, and the kingdom was virtually ruled by Northumberland. Foreseeing the death of Edward, he determined to snatch the crown away

from the Princess Mary, whose it would be lawfully and justly by right of succession, and retain it in his own family. To do this, it would
be necessary to make a tool of the king, and,
also, of Lady Jane Grey. It would be necessary,
first, to marry Lady Jane to his son, secondly, to
strengthen his own position by other marriages,
allying himself to eminent families, thirdly, to
coax Edward to bequeath the crown to Lady
Jane, or force him to do it, and finally, to conceal carefully his intentions from the virtuous
and innocent Lady Jane, whose whole nature
would rebel against the idea of an unjust usurpation of the crown until the last moment, when
through her love for her friends, and, especially,
her fear of her parents, and her devotion to Protestantism, she could be forced into accepting the
responsible part which was to be allotted to her
in this unfortunate drama. If Northumberland's
energy and talent had equalled his ambition,
there is no doubt but he might have succeeded
in his plans, for the cause of the Reformation
was loved by a large portion of the people, and
Lady Jane Grey was looked upon with affection
everywhere.

Northumberland determined to marry his

daughter, Lady Katharine, to Lord Hastings, eldest son of the Earl of Huntingdon; Lord Herbert eldest son of the earl of Pembroke, to Lady Katharine Grey, younger sister to Lady Jane; and his fourth son, Lord Guildford Dudley, to Lady Jane Grey. In the age of which we write it was not customary for parents to consult their children in reference to their matrimonial projects, and it is not probable that Lady Jane was consulted in reference to the marriage with Lord Guildford, her father, the duke of Suffolk, and Northumberland arranging the union with all its preliminaries. But the light of history is clear enough for us to discover that Lady Jane soon loved Dudley. He was scarcely twenty years of age, tall and graceful, and quite handsome, and well calculated to win the heart of the Lady Jane, who was almost a girl, and naturally very affectionate. The families had long been intimate, and it is likely that Guildford and Jane were well acquainted with each other; and possibly they were, before the marriage was spoken of, attached to each other. The courtship, however, was of short continuance, being consummated quickly by marriage It cannot be de-

nied that the marriage was planned by Northumberland and the Duke of Suffolk, and, at
least on their part, was a match of ambition, but
Guildford and Jane as yet knew nothing of the
proposed after-usurpation of the crown.

Walter Savage Landor—one of the most beautiful of the English authors—in his "*Imaginary
Conversations*" has one imaginary interview between Lady Jane, at this time, and her old
friend Roger Ascham. Although purely ficti-
tious, we will quote it here: —

Ascham.—Thou art going, my dear young
lady, into a most awful state; thou art passing
into matrimony and great wealth. God hath
willed it; submit in thankfulness. Thy affections are rightly placed and well distributed
Love is a secondary passion in those who love
most, a primary in those who love least. He
who is inspired by it in a high degree is inspired by honor in a higher; it never reaches
its plenitude of growth and perfection but in
the most exalted minds. Alas! alas!

Jane.—What aileth my virtuous Ascham?
Why do I tremble?

Ascham.—I remember a sort of prophesy,
made three years ago; it was the prophecy of

thy condition, and of my feelings on it. Recol
lectest thou who wrote, sitting upon the sea-
beach, the evening after an excursion to the
Isle of Wight, these verses?

> " Invisibly bright water ! so like air,
>   On looking down I feared thou couldst not bear
>   My little bark, of all light barks most light,
>   And looked again and drew me from the sight
>   And held the bench, not to go on so fast."

Jane.—I was very childish when I composed
them, and if I had thought any more about the
matter, I should have hoped that you would
have been too generous to keep them in your
memory as witnesses against me.

Ascham.—Nay, they are not so much amiss
for so young a girl, and there being so few of
them, I did not reprove thee. Half an hour I
thought might have been spent more unprofita-
bly; and I now shall believe it firmly, if thou
wilt be led by them to meditate a little on the
similarity of situations in which then thou wert,
to what thou art now in.

Jane.—I will do it and whatever else you
command, for I am weak by nature and very
timorous, unless where a strong sense of duty
holdeth and supporteth me. There God acteth,
and not his creatures. There were with me at

sea those who would have been attentive to me if I had seemed to be afraid, even though worshipful men and women were in the company; so that something more powerful threw my fear overboard. Yet I never will go again upon the water.

Ascham.—Exercise that beauteous couple, that mind and body, much and variously, but at home, at home, Jane! in-doors, and about things in-doors, for God is there too. We have rocks and quicksands on the banks of our Thames, O lady, such as ocean never heard of; and many —who knows how soon!—may be ingulphed in the current under their garden-walls.

Jane.—Thoroughly now do I understand you. Yes, indeed, I have read evil things of courts, but I think nobody can go out bad, who entereth good, if timely and true warning shall have been given.

Ascham.—I see perils on perils which thou dost not see, albeit thou art wiser than thy poor old master. And it is not because love hath blinded thee, for that surpasseth his supposed omnipotence; but it is because thy tender heart, having always leant affectionately upon good, hath felt and known nothing of evil. I

G

10

once persuaded thee to reflect muci , let me now persuade thee to avoid the habitude of reflection, to lay aside books, and to gaze care· fully and steadfastly on what is under and be fore thee.

Jane.—I have well bethought me of my duties. O how extensive they are! What a goodly and fair inheritance! But tell me, would you com· mand me never more to read Cicero, and Epicle· tus, and Polybus? The others I do resign: they are fit for the arbor and the gravel-walk: yet leave unto me, I beseech you, my friend and father, leave unto me for my fireside and for my pillow, truth, eloquence, courage, con· stancy.

Ascham.—Read them on thy marriage-bed, on thy child-bed, on thy death-bed. Thou spot· less, undrooping lily, they have fenced thee right well. These are the men for men; these are to fashion the bright and blessed creatures whom God shall one day smile upon in thy chaste bosom. Mind thou thy husband.

Jane.—I sincerely love the youth who hath espoused me; I love him with the fondest, the most solicitous affection. I pray to the Al· mighty for his goodness and happiness, and do

forget at times, unworthy suppliant, the prayers
I should have offered for myself. Never fear
that I will disparage my kind religious teacher,
by disobedience to my husband in the most
trying duties.

Ascham.—Gentle is he, gentle and virtuous;
but time will harden him: time must harden
even thee, sweet Jane! Do then complacently
and indirectly lead him from ambition.

Jane.—He is contented with me and with
home.

Ascham.—Ah, Jane! Jane! Men of high estate grow tired of contentedness.

Jane.—He told me he never liked books unless
I read them to him: I will read them to him
every evening: I will offer new worlds to him,
richer than those discovered by the Spaniards:
I will conduct him to treasures, O what treasures!
on which he may sleep in innocence and peace.

Ascham.—Rather do thou walk with him, ride
with him, play with him, be his fairy, his page,
his everything that love and poetry have invent-
ed; but watch him well, sport with his fancies,
turn them about like the ringlets round his cheek;
and if ever he meditateth on power, go toss up
thy baby to his brow, and bring back his

thoughts into his heart by the music of thy dis-
course.   Teach him to live unto God, and unto
thee; and he will discover that women, like the
plants in woods, derive their softness and tenderness from the shade."

During the last week of May, the marriage of
Lady Jane Grey with Lord Guildford Dudley
was celebrated at Durham House, in the Strand,
the residence of the Duke of Northumberland.
No more appropriate time could have been
chosen for the marriage of the innocent and lovely Lady Jane, than that of the English May. At
the same time and place, two other marriages
were solemnized—those of Lady Katharine Grey
with Lord Herbert, and Lady Katharine Dudley
with Lord Hastings.   The marriage ceremonies
of these illustrious weddings were conducted
magnificently, and a vast deal of show and pageantry were thrown about them.   It was very
proper that the day should be shrouded in solemnity, but the splendor of the occasion would
have passed unheeded, could those who took
part in the grand ceremonies only have looked
forward a few months into the future.   The
young king was pleased with the match of Lady
Jane, and it is said, that the last smiles which

graced his face were those seen there on this occasion. The court had already begun to put on the
hue of mourning, in its tone of feeling, in anticipa-
tion of Edward's death, but now, for a few days,
there was pomp and ceremony and general gladness. Edward ordered the master of the wardrobe to give to Lady Jane much wedding apparel,
as well as many jewels. Lady Jane, attired in a
dress embroidered with gold, between two pages,
and followed by a train of maidens, entered the
wedding apartment. When the ceremony was
performed, and it was known to the people in
the streets, there was a general rejoicing. Northumberland was hated by the people for his
terrible ambition, but they loved Lady Jane, and
could not dislike the young and harmless Dudley, her husband. The nuptials were celebrated
at court with great splendor, and for several
days there was general rejoicing and festivity.

As soon as the marriage ceremonies were fairly over, Lord Guildford and Lady Jane, the
summer being opened, retired to Sion House, a
seat of the Dudley family, to enjoy their honey-
moon. The spot was very beautiful, and the
season of the year was also charming, and without doubt the youthful couple here tasted a

happiness which was destined to be their last upon earth. Lady Jane wrote a third letter to Bullinger from this place, and it is preserved to this day in the library at Zurich.

Northumberland, who was constantly by the side of the king, saw that he now was declining so rapidly that he must execute his long contemplated schemes of aggrandizement and power. He first took care to gain the consent of the Duchess of Suffolk to transfer her own right of succession to her daughter Lady Jane. This was easily accomplished, though it was an unwarranted and effeminate proceeding. There now stood, in the event of Edward's death, which was absolutely certain, between Lady Jane Grey, Northumberland's daughter-in-law, but two personages—the Princesses Mary and Elizabeth. According to all the acknowledged principles of hereditary right, the first right of succession belonged to the Princess Mary, who was Henry VIII.'s eldest living child. But by her father's act, by act of Parliament, she had, together with the Princess Elizabeth, been bastardized. Henry had, however, in his will, made in 1544, given to Mary the right of succession. He passed by the right of the descendants of his older sister

Margaret to the crown, and placed next in order, as to the right of succession, the descendants of his younger sister Mary, Duchess of Suffolk. Northumberland saw that it would not do for him, upon the death of the king, to place Lady Jane upon the throne without special authority, for if the right really lay in the Brandon branch, the Duchess of Suffolk was the proper person to wear the crown. He, therefore, began to work upon the mind of the king to induce him to will his crown to Lady Jane Grey.

The king was a warm-hearted Protestant, and lying at the point of death, was an easy subject for an artful man to practise upon. The duke represented to him, that in case he did not make a will leaving the crown to Lady Jane, it would surely fall to the Princess Mary, who was a big oted Roman Catholic, and who would persecute those persons who were attached to the princi-ples of the Reformation. The Princess Elizabeth, who was a Protestant, must also be set aside, be-cause her father had by act of Parliament bas-tardized her, and if this act of bastardy were not acknowledged to be of force, neither could the same act against Lady Mary be binding; so, ac-cording to the reasoning of Northumberland, no

other course was open but to will the crown to
Lady Jane Grey. Yet a more reckless usurpation of the crown scarcely ever occurred. In
the hearts of the people everywhere, Catholic or
Protestant, there was a strong devotion to the
principles of hereditary right, and they would
not see the Princess Mary wronged. The same
feeling was in the heart of Lady Jane Grey, who
knew nothing of the mighty plans which were
in embryo, and which concerned herself more
closely than any other person in the kingdom.
It is not known whether the king was convinced
by the arguments of Northumberland, or so surrounded by his servants as to lack the courage
to deny him his wish, but he consented to make
a will. He at first supposed, of course, that he
was to bequeath the crown to Lady Suffolk, but
upon being told that she consented to relinquish
her right to her daughter Jane, Edward made no
objection to the change. Had he been usually
well, he must have detected the utter madness
of this scheme, for the Duchess of Suffolk was
yet liable to bear children, and in case she were
to have a son, he would indisputably have a right
to the throne. Thus deliberately was an avenue
left open to civil war.

The king first sketched with his own hand a
draft of the proposed entail of the crown, and
on the 11th of June sent for Sir Edward Mon-
tague, chief justice of the common pleas, Sir
Thomas Bromley, a puisne justice of the same·
court, Sir Richard Baker, chancellor of the aug-
mentations, and Goswold and Gryffyn, the attorney and solicitor-general, to attend the council at court. When they came he stated to
them what he had done, gave the reasons for
the proceeding, and wished them to draw up an
assignment of the crown to Lady Jane. They
replied that the act of Parliament settled the
succession, and they had no power over it. On
the 14th of June they again met the council,
when they declared to the king that they could
not execute his wish without subjecting themselves to the charge of treason. Northumberland was beside himself with rage, and swore
that he was ready to fight any man in so just a
cause, and declared afterwards he was ready
to have beaten these men. Such was the earnestness of the king, and the terrible anger of
Northumberland, that they at last consented to
draw up an assignment of the crown. There
was one exception. Hales, though a Protestant,

was so fully imbued with a sense of the injustice of the proceeding, that he refused to have any part in the matter. The will was prepared, engrossed on parchment, and had the great seal affixed to it. On the 21st of June it received the signature of the lords in council, of almost all of the judges, and of the attorney and solicitor-general. Twenty-four members of the council pledged their oaths to defend to the uttermost the will of the king, and if any man should ever attempt to alter it, to punish him as an enemy of the kingdom. The will in question asserted that Mary and Elizabeth were rendered incapable of inheriting the crown. It also declared that the descendants of Mary, sister of Henry VIII., were of the whole blood to Edward by the father's side, that they were " natural born within the realm, very honorably brought up, and exercised in good and godly learning, and other noble virtues, so that there is great trust and hope to be had in them that they be and shall be very well inclined to the advancement and setting forth of our common wealth."

The conclusion of the will was as follows : —

" The king doth, therefore, upon good deliberation and advice, herein had and taken, by these presents declare, order, assign, limit, and appoint, that if it shall fortune us to decease, leaving no issue of our body lawfully begotten, that then the said imperial crown and realm shall be unto the eldest son of the said Lady Frances, wife of the Duke of Suffolk and grand daughter of Henry VIII., lawfully begotten, being born into the world in our life-time, and to the heirs male of the said eldest son," etc., etc., and in default of which, "to the Lady Jane, eldest daughter of the said Lady Frances."

Archbishop Cranmer for a time refused to sign this will, indeed absented himself from council to avoid being asked, but the king sent to him and begged of him earnestly to do so, and he at length consented, though much against his own will. It was not that he loved Mary, or was particularly unwilling to bastardize her, but he had an affection for Elizabeth, who he well knew was at heart a warm Protestant. There were other notable men who signed the will with more or less unwillingness, and a few who would not consent to do it at all.

Edward now began to exhibit symptoms of immediate death. His breathing, which for a long time had been difficult, now grew still

worse; his pulse was scarcely perceptible; his
limbs swelled to an unusual size, and his countenance wore the livid hue of death.   There
was no feeling of disappointment in those around
the orphan-king; indeed, the feeling of sorrow
had lost its poignancy, from the fact that his
death had been considered as a settled event,
soon to occur, for many months.   The majority
of the court were creatures of Northumberland,
and they well knew that their master expected to
found his fortunes upon the decease of the king;
—it could not be expected that *they* should
mourn Edward's demise.   But there was a large
class who felt the most poignant sorrow at the
calamity which in a few days was to befall the
nation. They were men who loved the principles
of the Reformation, and who also loved justice.
Edward was, though young, a true-hearted Protestant, and if he had lived, would have been a
friend to liberty, literature, and an enlightened
religion.   The greatest possible contrast existed
between his reign and that of his father, Henry
VIII.   The one was ferocious, blood-thirsty, and
irreligious, though pretending to a love for good
things.   The other was mild almost to ineffi-
ciency, gentle as a girl, full of lovely piety, and

fond of classic literature. Under Henry the
nation held its breath for fear; under Edward
it was free and happy, notwithstanding the in-
numerable insurrections and commotions, which
were partly a result of Henry's previous tyranny,
and the wretched statesmanship of Edward's
ministers.

When the month of July was ushered in, it
became certain that Edward could survive but a
few days. His physicians declared that they
could do no more for him. He was given over
to the care of a miserable female quack, and
sunk with alarming rapidity to his grave. The
6th day of July was his last day upon earth.
In the evening of that day, while engaged in
prayer, calm and fearless as a saint, the gentle
prince expired, having lived nearly sixteen years,
and reigned six years and five months.

CHAPTER VIII.

THE PRINCESS MARY.—HER EARLY MORTIFICATIONS. —HER DISGRACE.
—FRUITLESS ATTEMPTS AT MARRIAGE.—NORTHUMBERLAND'S TREAT-
MENT OF MARY.—REMARKS UPON HER CHARACTER.

IT will be proper for us here to give a short sketch of that princess who was the legitimate successor to Edward VI., and by whose hand Lady Jane Grey met her fate. Unless Queen Mary's previous history is taken into account, the reader will scarcely be able to understand the secret of her severe, and oftentimes heartless conduct. The Princess Mary was born at Greenwich Palace on February 18th, 1516, and was consequently, upon the death of Edward, nearly thirty-eight years of age. She was the daughter of Henry VIII. by Katharine of Arragon. When only six years old she was betrothed to the Emperor Charles V., and she was, accordingly, educated for a brilliant position. Three years after this, rumors came to England that the emperor

meant to desert Mary, and was already engaged
to Isabel of Portugal. Mary grew pale with jealousy, though only eight years of age, which
certainly indicated a frightful precocity of the
passions. A year after the emperor married
Isabel. This was the first of a long series of disappointments in her life, every one of which was
calculated to inflict the severest wound upon a
woman's nature. At this period of her life she
was the heiress to the crown of England, and was
called the Princess of Wales. She was a lovely
child, being obedient, intelligent, and cheerful in
her disposition. Francis I. of France at this
time entered into negotiations respecting Mary,
but finally married Eleanora. He professed after
this a desire to marry his son Henry to the princess Mary, but about this time, the doubts in
reference to her legitimacy were first broached,
and her matrimonial projects were rendered
hopeless. Henry VIII. separated from his wife,
and declared Mary to be the offspring of an incestuous marriage. No keener mortification
could it possibly have been Mary's lot to feel,
and it is a wonder that she did not go mad.
To add to her sorrow, she was torn from her
mother's arms, to behold her again no more

This cruel act could only have been perpetrated by a monster. Her mother wrote to her, for she was truly a blessed woman, and endeavored to cheer her with hopes of brighter days in the future. It was not until the birth of Elizabeth that Henry completely disinherited Mary. At the age of seventeen, Mary came to court to witness the ceremonies surrounding the birth of Elizabeth. Henry required that she should greet the new born princess according to her rank, as heir to the crown, but she refused. "Sister, I will call the babe," said she, "but nothing more." Henry threatened, but Mary was firm, for she would not consent, at that time, to acknowledge her mother's disgrace. The privy council commanded her to lay aside the title of princess, and demanded that her own servants should not ad dress her by any title. During this year, James V. became suitor for the hand of Mary, notwith standing her situation, but his suit was refused by the king peremptorily. In the beginning of 1534, her disgrace was made complete by act of Parliament, which took away from her her rights and titles, and declared her to be an illegitimate child. Her establishment was broken up, and she was taken from her dear old friend the

Countess of Salisbury, and was transferred to an apartment in the household of the princess Elizabeth. This was heaping insult upon injury. If the heart of Mary was not soured by such cruel treatment, by such misfortunes which thickly clustered in her path, she was an exception, and a remarkable one, among her sex.

When Mary was twenty years old her mother died. She begged the privilege of kissing her lips in death, of taking one farewell look of the being who had brought her into the world, but her wish was cruelly refused. This treatment proceeded from a man who professed dissatisfaction with the Romish religion, and it only tended to render Mary still more intense in her devotion to that church which had defended her, and ooldly declared the wrongs which her mother had suffered.

The death of a male heir at this time gave the friends of Mary more hope, and the new queen, Jane Seymour, seems to have looked upon her with some affection. Mary began to hope for a place again in her father's heart, but the king told her that the price of her restoration to court must be her acknowledgment that her mother's marriage was incestuous. At

11

first she bitterly rebelled against such a require-
ment, but upon consideration she thought it
politic to sign her own disgrace, hoping that
when she was received into the society of her
father, she might win him to grant her a portion
of her natural rights. She loved the king, it is
said,—though how this can have been true we
cannot conceive,—and was exceedingly desirous
of seeing him. She was, also, without any judi-
cious friend to guide her, and finally consented
to acknowledge that the marriage of her mother
was incestuous, and consequently that her own
birth was illegitimate. It is impossible to apol-
ogize for this disgraceful act. Mary believed
the marriage of her mother to have been a most
righteous, though very unfortunate one, had not
the slightest doubts in reference to her own
legitimate birth, yet she deliberately consented
to belie her own dearest convictions, to cover
with shame the memory of a pious mother, for
the sake of peace with the king. We can account for this act only upon the ground that by
repeated misfortunes and mortifications Mary's
heart had become hardened, and that she did
not look upon the disgrace of illegitimacy with
so much horror as she had done a few years

before. The following is a copy of the remarkable acknowledgment of her own degradation :—

"LADY MARY'S SUBMISSION.

"The confession of me, the Lady Mary, made
upon certain points and articles under written,
in the which, as I do now plainly and with all
mine heart confer and declare mine inward sentence, belief, and judgment, with a due conform-
ity of obedience to the laws of the realm, so
minding ever to persist and continue in this
determination, without change, alteration, or va-
riance, I do most humbly beseech the king's
highness, my father, whom I have obstinately
and *inobediently* offended, in the denial of the
same heretofore, to forgive my offences therein,
and to take me to his most gracious mercy.

" First, I confess and acknowledge the king's
majesty to be my sovereign lord and king, in the
imperial crown of this realm of England, and to
submit to his highness, and to all and singular
laws and statutes of this realm, as becometh a true
and faithful subject to do, which I shall obey,
keep, observe, advance, and maintain, according
to my bounden duty, with all the power, force,

and qualities that God hath indued me, during my life.   (Signed)   MARY.

"Item. I do recognize, accept, take, repute, and acknowledge the king's highness to be supreme head in earth under Christ, of the Church of England, and do utterly refuse the bishop of Rome's pretended authority, power, and jurisdiction, within this realm heretofore usurped, according to the laws and statutes made in that behalf, and of all the king's true subjects humbly received, admitted, obeyed, kept, and observed; and also do utterly renounce and forsake all manner of remedy, interest, and advantage which I may by any means claim by time, or in any wise hereafter, by any manner, title color, mean, or case that is, shall or can be devised for that purpose.   (Signed)   MARY.

"Item. I do freely, frankly, and for the discharge of my duty towards God, the king's highness, and his laws, without other respect, recognize and acknowledge that the marriage heretofore had between his majesty and my mother, the late princess-dowager, was by God's law and man's law, incestuous and unlawful.

(Signed)   " MARY."

Mary's household was now established upon a comfortable footing, and in the autumn overtures were made for her marriage with Henry, Duke of Orleans. The king even hinted that she might be restored to her right of succession. It is supposed by some historians that at this time Mary loved the celebrated Reginald Pole, and that she intended one day to marry him. But Henry continued to negotiate for her marriage with foreign princes, all of his plans proving unsuccessful. A life more mortifying cannot be conceived than that which the Lady Mary led, for she was literally a-begging over Europe for a husband. When she was twenty-two years old an attempt was made to marry her to the Duke of Cleves, and her portrait was sent into Saxony for the purpose, but all negotiations failed of their intent. The next proposed alliance was with the Duke of Bavaria, but by Henry's treatment of Anne of Cleves, this match was broken off. In the year 1540 Mary's old schoolmaster, a zealous Catholic, suffered martyrdom for his religion. Then her dear old friend, the Countess of Salisbury, met with a horrible end. The result was that Mary imbibed a hatred of the Reformers which she was

destined one day to gratify by still more horrible deeds.

When Henry VIII. married Katharine, he
restored his daughter Mary to her royal rank,
and when he died, in his will he restored her to
her proper place in the succession, and gave her
a marriage portion of £10,000.

When Dudley—afterwards Northumberland
—came to power, he commenced a system of
persecution against the Princess Mary on account of her devotion to the Romish religion.
Her chaplains were arrested, and the council
determined that she should not perform mass
in her chapel. But Mary was now bigoted in
her devotion to her religion, and would not give
up her religious rights. She came to court and
had an interview with Edward, declaring her
willingness, if need be, to lay down her life.
She was now nervous, querulous, soured, and
possessed of a temper which she could not at all
times control. She therefore endured the vexa-
tious proceedings of Northumberland with much
impatience. It was her conduct at this time
which led Edward to consent to will the crown
to Lady Jane Grey, who was a sincere Protestant.

When Edward expired, the Princess Mary was nearly thirty-eight years of age, and unmarried. At the early age of six years she had been betrothed, and at eight was cast off by her royal lover. Thus it will be seen that she scarcely entered upon life before she was doomed to mortification. By the injudicious treatment of her teachers, she was at eight led to love a man much her senior in years, so that his breach of engagement actually had a bad effect upon her health! Doomed next to be separated from her mother, and still later to be accused of illegitimacy, and forced—she, the proud daughter of a king—to acknowledge her shameful condition, and, through her whole life, to negotiations for marriage with an indefinite number of persons, all of which projects fell short of success— is it any wonder that now we behold her a broken-hearted, crushed, almost ruined woman? The father of Lady Jane Grey had used his talents and influence to crush Katharine of Arragon, mother to the Princess Mary. He had favored the divorce, favored the degradation of that pious queen and her innocent daughter and Mary hated him, and hated his children Northumberland, too, had taken every sure method of rousing her vindictiveness, whenever she could exercise it with safety. He had arrested her chaplains, interfered in her style of worship, and in short rendered himself odious to her. Lady Jane Grey was his daughter-in-law —that alone were enough to decide her fate, in case she fell into Mary's power on a charge of treason, especially if on a charge of usurpation of the crown, which was a right now belonging to Mary.

It is impossible to excuse the conduct which characterized the whole of Queen Mary's reign, and the present chapter is not an apology for her blood-thirsty persecutions, but merely an attempt to show the reader how Mary had become hardened—how she had lost that loveliness of character which was in reality hers when she was young. She was now, it cannot be denied, a cold-hearted, bigoted woman. Insulted, spurned, trodden under foot all her life, she felt willing to revenge herself upon the world for its cruel treatment of herself. That she was a pious woman we believe, but she was astonishingly bigoted and fanatical, and consequently a most dangerous person to sit upon the throne of England. More precocious in her passions than her intellect, she was, at the age of thirty-eight, an unpleasant woman, to say the least, for an intimate companion, and well fitted to act the part of a persecutor. Yet Mary must not be made responsible for all the terrible deeds which occurred during her reign. In many, perhaps the majority of instances, she was persuaded by cruel ministers to destroy life, and often she may be said scarcely to have known anything of the diabolical tortures to which some of the Protestants were put. There were occasions, too, in which she exhibited signs of the most tender feeling, proving that the heart which in her youth was filled with the gentlest attributes, could not ever quite lose its original character. But we must hurry on to the course of our narrative.

CHAPTER IX.

THE first thing which Northumberland attempted to do after the death of the king, was
to conceal that fact from the nation for a few
days, to enable him the more surely to establish Lady Jane Grey upon the throne, and to
take possession of the Princess Mary, who had
been summoned to attend the death-bed of the
king. As soon as Edward had expired, the
Duke of Northumberland, accompanied by the
Duke of Suffolk, Earl of Pembroke, and other
noblemen, proceeded to Sion House, and acknowledged Lady Jane Grey to be their queen.
This seems to have been the first time that Lady

Jane had any definite idea in reference to the
bestowment of the crown upon herself. Until
now, she had been kept in perfect ignorance of
the ambitious designs of Northumberland and
her father, the Duke of Suffolk. True to her
conscientious nature, she refused to take the
crown thus offered to her! To her there was
no pleasure in the contemplation of a brilliant
career as Queen of England. She was too gentle, too pious for a courtly life. And when they
came to press upon her that crown, which was to
her a crown of thorns, she was with her young
lord, enjoying his caresses amid the retired but
beautiful lands of Sion House. Her father ex-
plained to her that Edward VI., who had just
expired, had bequeathed the crown to her, that
the privy council were unanimously of opinion
that she was the lawful heir to the throne, and
that the people of London were of the same
opinion. The young bride was at first astonished by their representations, and when Northumberland, her father, and other distinguished
noblemen fell at her feet, was almost bewildered.
But she soon calmly answered them in nearly
the following words :—

"The laws of the kingdom and natural right

stand for the king's sisters, and I will beware of
burthening a weak conscience with a yoke
which belongeth to them; I understand the
infamy of those who permit the violation of
right, to gain a sceptre; and it is mocking God
and deriding justice, to scruple at the stealing of
a shilling, and not at the usurpation of a crown.
Besides, I am not so young, nor so little read in
the guiles of fortune, to suffer myself to be taken
by them. If she enrich any, it is but to make
them the subject of her spoil; if she raise others,
it is but to pleasure herself with their ruins;
what she adorned but yesterday, is to-day her
pastime; and if I now permit her to adorn and
crown me, I must to-morrow suffer her to crush
and tear me to pieces. Nay, with what crown
doth she present me? A crown which hath been
violently and shamefully wrested from Katharine of Arragon, made more unfortunate by the
punishment of Anne Boleyn, and others that
wore it after her; and why, then, would you
have me add my blood to theirs, and be the
third victim from whom this fatal crown may
be ravished, with the head that wears it? But
even in case that it should not prove fatal unto
me, and that all its venom were consumed, if

fortune should give me warranties of her constancy, should I be well advised to take upon
me these thorns, which would not fail to torment me, though I were assured not to be stran-
gled with it? My liberty is better than the
chain you offer me, with what precious stones
soever it be adorned, or of what gold soever
framed. I will not exchange my peace for honorable and precious jealousies, for magnificent
and glorious fetters, and if you love me sincerely
and in good earnest, you will rather wish me a
secure and quiet fortune, though mean, than an
exalted condition exposed to the wind, and followed by some dismal fall."

We are sure that the reader will coincide with
us in the opinion that a more touching and eloquent reply could not have been made by Lady
Jane. Her prophetic words in reference to her
"dismal fall" were remembered long after her
mistake had been expiated upon the scaffold.

Northumberland and the Duke of Suffolk
again represented to Lady Jane, with vehement
earnestness, that the crown was of right hers,
and also laid fully before her the dreadful con-
sequences which would result to the Protestant
party if she refused to accept it, and thus con-

tribute to the rise to power of a vindictive
Catholic. Lady Jane had been educated to believe that to disobey a father's command was an
almost atrocious act. She had been accustomed
always to obey, to give up her own will to that
of others. Her parents were always severe in
their education, and she was poorly fitted to
withstand the express command of her father.
He did not now hesitate to insist that she take
the crown. But finally her own husband used
his eloquence to persuade her to mount the
throne. It is probable that before this he was
aware of Lady Jane's brilliant prospects; at any
rate, now his heart was fired with ambition,
and he sank upon his knees before his young
and gentle bride, and begged of her not to
refuse the gorgeous bauble. It is said that at
last not merely eloquence was used by her
friends to persuade her to take the fearful step,
but that threats were used until she, exhausted
with weeping and frightful agitation, sank to
the floor in a fainting fit.

Lady Jane was only sixteen; gentle, broken
in spirit; and now her father commanded, her
husband entreated, her councillors advised, that
she consent to become the Queen of England

Her love for Protestantism was touched; she was threatened with the loss of the love of her dear-est friends—is it strange that she became a pas-sive victim in their hands? Such was the fact. From this time to her death she was really a prisoner—first in the hands of her friends, and lastly in the hands of her enemies. Alas! her friends were her worst enemies.

On the 8th of July, Lady Jane appointed Lord Clinton constable of the Tower. This was the first acknowledgment of her power, by herself, and this act was in reality Northumberland's, for he controlled the queen. On the 9th, the supe-rior officers of the guard at Greenwich took oaths of allegiance to Lady Jane. The same day the Bishop of London preached a powerful sermon at St. Paul's, in favor of Lady Jane's acceptance of the crown. In the afternoon of the 10th of July, Lady Jane openly assumed a royal state and the government of the realm.

But it will be necessary for us to recount the movements of the Princess Mary and her friends at this time.

Northumberland concealed the death of Ed-ward, and sent for Mary to come and see her dying brother. His object was to gain possession of her person. She started for Greenwich, but at Hoddesden she met a messenger who declared to her that Edward was dead. She could hardly believe the man, and very much feared it was a trap laid for her by her enemies. For if she were to assert herself Queen of England, if it should afterwards appear that Edward was yet alive, she would expose herself to the pains of treason. Sir Nicolas Throckmorton sent the messenger to her; Sir Robert, his brother, had long been her devoted adherent, and she said:

"If Robert had been at Greenwich I would have hazarded all things, and gaged my life on the leap." She staid that night near Cambridge, at the house of a Mr. Huddleston, and in the morning proceeded towards Kenninghall. When upon the summit of a mountain she looked back and saw the house in which she had lodged in flames. Her enemies had done the deed. "Let it blaze," said Mary, "I will build Huddleston a better!" On the 9th, at Kenninghall, Mary addressed a letter to the privy council, offering pardon to them if they would proclaim her their sovereign. This letter was received on the morning of the 10th, and Northumberland at once proclaimed Lady Jane Grey Queen of England. The custom had always been for a new sovereign to spend the few first days of a reign at the Tower, and Lady Jane left Sion House for Durham House, in London, and from that place proceeded by boats to the Tower. It was between four and five o'clock in the afternoon when she entered that palace and prison. She was followed by a numerous retinue, consisting of the nobility of either sex, and her train was borne up by her own mother, assisted by other ladies of the highest rank. The ordnance of the Tower saluted the cavalcade, and when Lady Jane had entered, the Marquis of Winchester brought to her the crown. But she only wept sorrowfully, and lifted not a finger to place it upon her head, but passively waited for others to hold it there. At the outset of her short reign she seems to have been oppressed by a terrible weight of sorrow, so as to render her scarcely capable of any action. It is probble that she foresaw the result of all this pageantry.

As soon as Lady Jane was crowned in the Tower, a proclamation was issued; at six o'clock, heralds with a trumpet announced the same to

the people, claiming their allegiance. The mass
of the people an hour before were in utter ignorance of Edward's death, and they received the
proclamation with coolness. It was the same
everywhere; the people were not in favor of
the usurpation of the crown, but dared not
oppose it. Lady Jane was beloved, and Protestantism was beloved, by the English, but they
loved dearer yet the right of succession, and
could not see that law of right broken. Besides
this, the people hated intensely the Duke of
Northumberland, and were fully aware that
Lady Jane was his victim. The Duke was
overbearing in his disposition, ambitious, reckless, and a tyrant. Oppression from the hands
of a legitimate monarch was pleasanter to them
than the rule of an upstart, who would make a
tool of the Queen Jane. It is said that Lady
Jane noticed that in the streets she was not
greeted with any enthusiasm, and turning to her
husband, called his attention to the perilous fact.
From this moment Mary's adherents were hope-
ful, for the people at heart were on her side.
We give the proclamation of the queen, with
the exception of a few unimportant para-
graphs :

"PROCLAMATION.

"JANE, by the grace of God Queen of England, France, and Ireland, Defender of the Faith
and of the Church of England, and also of Ireland, under Christ on earth the supreme head.
To all our loving, faithful, and obedient subjects,
to every of them, greeting. Whereas our most
dear cousin, Edward the Sixth, late King of
England, France, and Ireland, Defender of the
Faith, and on earth the supreme head, under
Christ, of the Church of England and Ireland,
by his letters patent, signed with his own hand,
and sealed with his great seal of England, bearing date the 21st day of June, in the 7th year of
his reign, in the presence of the most part of his
nobles, his counsellors, judges, and divers other
grave and sage personages, etc., etc. * * * *
* * * * *   Forasmuch as the imperial
crown of this realm, by an act made in the
thirty-fifth year of the reign of King Henry the
Eighth, our projenitor and great uncle, for lack
of issue of his body lawfully begot, and for lack
of issue of the body of our said late cousin, King
Edward the Sixth, by the same act limited and
appointed to remain to the Lady Mary, by the
name of the Lady Mary, his eldest daughter,

and to the heirs of her body lawfully begot, and
for the default of such issue the remainder thereof to the Lady Elizabeth, by the name of the
Lady Elizabeth, his second daughter, and to the
heirs of her body lawfully begotten, with such
conditions as should be limited and appointed
by the said late king of worthy memory, King
Henry the Eighth, our progenitor and great
uncle, by his letters patents under the great seal,
or by his last will in writing, signed with his
hand.   And forasmuch as the said limitation of
the imperial crown of this realm, being limited
as is aforesaid, to the said Lady Mary and Lady
Elizabeth, being illegitimate and not lawfully begotten, for that the marriage had between the
said late king, Henry the Eighth, our projenitor and great uncle, and the Lady Katharine,
mother to the said Lady Mary; and also the
marriage had between the said late king, Henry
the Eighth, our progenitor and great uncle, and
the Lady Anne, mother to the said Lady Elizabeth, were clearly and lawfully undone by sentences of divorces, according to the word of
God, and the ecclesiastical laws, and which said
several divorcements have been severally ratified
and confirmed by authority of Parliament, and

especially in the thirty-third year of the reign
of King Henry the Eighth, our progenitor and
great uncle, remaining in force, strength, and
effect, whereby as well the said Lady Mary, as
also the said Lady Elizabeth, to all intents and
purposes are and be thereby disabled to ask,
claim, or challenge the said imperial crown, or
any other of the honors, castles, manors, lordships, lands, tenements, or other hereditaments,
as heir or heirs to our said late cousin, King
Edward the Sixth, or as heir or heirs to any
other person or persons whosoever, as well for
the causes before rehearsed, as also for that the
said Ladys Mary and Elizabeth were unto our
said late cousin but of the half blood, and therefore by the ancient laws, statutes, and customs of
this realm, be not inheritable unto our said late
cousin, although they had been born in lawful
matrimony, as indeed they were not, as by the
said sentences of divorce, and the said statute of
the twenty-eighth year of the reign of our king,
Henry the Eighth, our said progenitor and great
uncle, plainly appeareth; and forasmuch, also, as
it is to be thought, or at least must be doubted,
that if the said Lady Mary or Lady Elizabeth
should hereafter have and enjoy the said impe-

rial crown of this realm, and should happen to
marry with any stranger out of this realm, that
the said stranger, having the government and
imperial crown in his hands, would adhere and
practise, not only to bring this noble free realm
into the tyranny and servitude of the Bishop of
Rome, but also to the laws and customs of his
or their own native country or countries, to be
practised and be put in use within this realm,
rather than the laws, statutes, and customs, here
of long time used, whereupon the title of inheritance of all and singular the subjects of this
realm do depend, to the peril of conscience, and
the utter subversion of the common weal of this
realm. Whereupon our said late dear cousin,
weighing and considering with himself what
ways and means were most convenient to be
had for the stay of the said succession in the
said imperial crown, if it should please God to
call our said late cousin out of this transitory
life, having no issue of his body, and calling to
his remembrance that we, and the Lady Katharine and the Lady Marie, our sisters, being the
daughters of the Lady Frances, our natural mother, and then and yet wife to our natural and most
loving father, Henry, Duke of Suffolk, and the

Lady Margaret, daughter of the Lady Eleanore, then deceased, sister to the said Lady Frances, and the late wife of our cousin Henry, Earl of Cumberland, were very nigh of his grace's blood, of the part of his father's side, our said progenitor and great uncle, and being naturally born here within the realm, and for the very good opinion our said late cousin had of our and our said sisters and cousin Margaret's good education, did therefore, upon good deliberation and advice, herein had and taken, by his said letters patents declare, order, assign, limit, and appoint, that if it should fortune himself, our said late cousin, King Edward the Sixth, to decease, leaving no issue of his body lawfully begotten, that then the said imperial crown of England and Ireland, and the confines of the same, and his title to the crown of the realm of France, and all and singular honors, castles, prerogatives, privileges, preliminaries, authorities, jurisdictions, dominions, possessions, and hereditaments, to our said late cousin, King Edward the Sixth, or to the said imperial crown belonging, or in anywise appertaining, should, for lack of such issue of his body, remain, come, and be unto the eldest son of the body of the said Lady Frances, lawfully

begotten, and so from son to son, as he should be
of authentic birth, of the body of the said Lady
Frances lawfully begotten, being born into the
world in our said cousin's lifetime, and to the
heirs male of the body of every such son lawfully begotten; and for default of such son born
into the world in his lifetime, of the body of the
said Lady Frances, lawfully begotten, and for lack
of heirs male of every such son lawfully begotten, that then the said imperial crown, and a.'
and singular other the premises should remain
come, and be to us, by the name of the Lady
Jane, eldest daughter of the said Lady Frances
and to the heirs male of our body lawfully be
gotten, that then the said imperial crown, and
all other the premises, shall remain, come, and
be to the said Lady Katharine, our said second
sister, and to the heirs male of the body of the
said Lady Katharine lawfully begotten, with
divers other remainders, as by the same letters
patent more plainly at large it may and doth
appear. Since the making of which letters
patent, that is to say, on Thursday, which was
the sixth day of this instant month of July, it
has pleased God to call to his infinite mercy our
said most dear and entirely beloved cousin,

Edward the Sixth, whose soul God pardon, and forasmuch as he is now deceased, having no heirs of his body begotten, and that also there remaineth at this present time no heirs lawfully begotten of the body of our said progenitor and great uncle, King Henry the Eighth; and forasmuch also as the said Lady Frances, our said mother, had no issue male begotten of her body, and born into the world in the lifetime of our said cousin, King Edward the Sixth, so as the said imperial crown, and other the premises to the same belonging, or in anywise appertaining, now be and remain to us in our actual and royal possession, by authority of the said letters patent: We do, therefore, by these presents, signify unto all our most loving, faithful and obedient subjects, that like as we for our part shall, by God's grace, show ourselves a most gracious and benign sovereign queen and lady to all our good subjects, in all their just and lawful suits and causes, and to the uttermost of our power shall preserve and maintain God's most holy word, Christian polity, and the good laws, customs, and liberties of these our realms and dominions: so we mistrust not, but they and every of them, will again for their parts, at a'l times, and in all cases, show themselves unto us, their natural liege queen and lady, most faithful, loving, and obedient subjects, according to their bounden duties and allegiances, whereby they shall please God, and do the thing that shall tend to their own preservation and security; willing and commanding all men of all estates, degrees, and conditions, to see our peace and accord kept, and to be obedient to our laws, as they tender our favor, and will answer for the contrary at their extreme peril.

"In witness whereof we have caused these our letters to be made patent.

"Witness ourself, at our Tower of London, this tenth day of July, in the first year of our reign.

"GOD SAVE THE QUEEN."

This proclamation was read to the inhabitants of London, and as we have remarked, excited no enthusiasm. It fell coldly upon their ears, for they knew every word came direct from the ambitious brain of Northumberland. They saw, too, that its reasoning was fallacious; they could not resist the conviction that Mary, however repugnant in her character and religious princi-

ples to them, was nevertheless the lawful queen
of the realm. Yet no opposition was made,
with a single exception, to the assumption of the
crown by Lady Jane. The exception was the
case of a young man apprentice to a vintner,
who asserted Mary's rights aloud, and as a punishment for his offence he was set on the pillory,
and had both of his ears cut off.

Queen Jane, though residing in the Tower,
made preparations for a removal in a few weeks.
She appointed Sir Ambrose Dudley to be keeper
of her palace at Westminster, who began to
make preparations for the queen's change of
residence. On the 11th of July the council
wrote to commissioners, then in Flanders to negotiate a treaty of peace, the following despatch :

"After our hearty commendations, ye shall
learn by this bearer, Mr. Shelley, and by such
letters as ye shall receive from the queen's highness, our sovereign lady, Queen Jane, which
copy of such letters as are hers ye are to send to
the emperor, which is the cause of this message
now sent to you, and what it is that is now to
be done by you there; first, the signification of
our lord's death ; next, the possession of the
queen's highness in the crown of this realm;

thirdly, the placing of you, Sir Phillip Hobbye, knight, as ambassador there resident; fourthly and last, the offer for your remaining there to proceed in the treaty of peace, if it shall so like the emperor. Furthermore, ye shall understand that although the Lady Mary hath been neither to write us to remain quiet, yet nevertheless we see her not so weigh the matter, that if she might she would disturb the state of this realm, having thereunto as yet no manner apparent of help or comfort but only the cognizance of a few lords and base people, all other the nobility and gentlemen remaining in their duties to our sovereign lady, Queen Jane. And yet, nevertheless, because the conditions of the baser sort of people is understood to be unruly if they be not governed and kept in order, therefore for the meeting with all events, the Duke of Northumberland's grace, accompanied with the Lord Marquis of Northampton, proceedeth with a convenient power into the parties of Norfolk, to keep those countries in stay and obedience; and 'because the emperor's ambassadors here remaining shall on this matter of the policy not intermeddle, as it is very likely they will and do dispose, the Lord Cobham and Sir John Mason repair-eth to the same ambassadors to give them notice of the Lady Mary's proceedings against the state of this realm, and to put them in remem. brance of the nature of their office, which is not to meddle in these causes of policy, neither directly or indirectly, and so to charge them to use themselves as they give no occasion of unkindness to be ministered unto them, whereas we would be most sorry for the amity which on our part we mean to conserve and maintain. And for that grace the ambassadors here shall advertise thither what is said to them. Ye shall therefore declare to the emperor both the cause of this message to his ambassadors, and what the very message is, using it in such sort as thereby the amity may best be preserved.

"The 11th of July, 1553. The Council to the Commissioners."

The queen's despatch (really prepared by the council) was as follows :

"JANE THE QUEEN.

"Trusty and well-beloved,—We greet you well. It hath so pleased God of his providence, by the calling of our most dear cousin of famous memory, King Edward the Sixth, out of this

life, to our very natural sorrow, that we be, both
by our said cousin's lawful determination in his
lifetime, with the assent of the nobility and state
of this our realm, and also as his lawful heir
and successor in the whole blood royal, possessed of this our realm of England and Ireland.
Wherefore we have presently sent to our good
brother, the emperor, this present bearer hereof,
our trusty servant, Mr. Richard Shelley, with
letters of recommendation and credence from us,
thereby signifying unto him as well the sorrowful death of our said cousin the king, as also our
succession in the crown of this realm, motioning
unto our good brother the continuance in such
amity and league as our said cousin and prede-
cessor had with him, for which purpose we have
furthermore signified by our said letters, not
only our orders that you, Sir Phillip Hobbye,
shall there remain and rest with our said good
brother the emperor, as our ambassador resident,
praying him to give you credit appertaining to
such an office, but also that for the like zeal and
desire we have to the weal of Christendom, as
our said cousin King Edward had, wherein we
do count to follow his steps, we have given
order that ye, the whole number of our ambas-

sadors, shall there remain to continue to dwell
in the former commission which ye had from
our ancestor the king, if it shall please our said
good brother, the copy of which our letters we
send to you herewith, for your more ample
understanding of our determination, which considered and pondered we would ye made the
most speedy course to our said good brother,
and in order to execute the matters contained in
the said letters of your part to be declared—first,
the signification of the death of our said ancestor
and cousin the king, whereof as we by nature
must take great grief, so we doubt not but our
said good brother will, for friendship and great
amity, sorrow and condole with us; next, that
you, Sir Phillip Hobbye, have express order
there to reside and attend upon our good brother
as our minister, for the continuance and the en-
tertainment of the intelligence and firm amity
heretofore had and concluded betwixt our said
ancestor and cousin the king and our said good
brother, the maintenance whereof we, with the
assent of our nobility and council, do much desire, and for our pity will not fail but confirm·
and maintain the same. In third, ye shall show
to our said good brother that as we do by God's

good providence succeed to our said ancestor
and cousin, King Edward the Sixth, in this
our crown and dominions, so do we also find
in our heart and mind the very descent and
inheritance of his most Christian devotion and
affection to the common weal of Christendom,
which moveth us, with the advice of our nobility and council, to offer to our said good brother
the ministry and office of you our ambassadors,
to remain there and proceed in the former commission for the consolation of some good peace
betwixt our said good brother and the French
king, wherein we refer our good purpose and
meaning to the mind and contentation of our
said good brother. This done. whatsoever our
good brother shall answer ye may thereunto
reply as ye think expedient, tending to the continuance of our ancestor's amity, with an addi-
tion that ye forthwith report unto us. For the
rest of the proceeding hereof, ye shall understand by the bearer, to whom we would ye
should give credit.

"Given under our signate, at our Tower of
London, 11th July, 1553."

The following address by Queen Jane to cer-

tain of her nobility, was prepared by Northumberland at this time, and the original draft
still remains in the British Museum. In certain places, sentences or parts of sentences are
lost : —

"Right trusty and well-beloved councillors—
We greet you well, and desire the same, that
whereas it hath pleased Almighty God to call
to his mercy out of this life, our dearest cousin
the king, your late sovereign lord. By reason
whereof, and such ordinances as the said late
king did establish in his lifetime, for the security and welfare of this realm, we are entered into
our rightful possession of this kingdom, as by
the last will of our said dearest cousin, our late
ancestor, and other several instruments to that
effect, signed with his own hand, and sealed
with the great seal of this realm England * * *
in his own presence, and the nobles of this
realm for the most part, and all our council
and judges, with the * * * * here also sub-
scribed their names, as by the same will and
testament it may now evidently and doth appear; now, therefore, do you understand that
by the * * * and sufferance of the heavenly
Lord, and by the assent and consent of the said

I
13

nobles and councillors, and others before signified, we do this day make our entry into our
Tower of London, as rightful queen of this
realm, and have accordingly set forth our proclamation to all our loving subjects, giving them
thereby to understand the same as their duty
of allegiance which they now of right owe unto
us, as most amply shall be shown hereafter,
nothing doubting, right trusty and well-beloved
councillors, but that you will endeavor yourselves in all things to the uttermost of your
power, not only to defend for our use, but also
assist us in our rightful possession of this kingdom, and to disturb, repel, and resist the feigned
and untrue claim of the Lady Mary, bastard
daughter to our great uncle, Henry the Eighth,
of famous memory. Wherein as you shall, and
that what to your truth and duty appertain-
eth, so shall we grant and show unto you and
yours accordingly."

Neither of the preceding papers purporting to
emanate from the queen, really were prepared
by Lady Jane, and it is doubtful if she saw
them. The ostensible head of the kingdom was
in truth an innocent girl, who was a prisoner of
the Duke of Northumberland. The duke pro-

fessed to feel thoroughly at his ease in reference
to the state of the kingdom, but his dispatches
reveal the truth—that he was alarmed, and exceedingly anxious to win confidence from the
nobility, and countenance from the German emperor. His subsequent conduct fully proved
that he never had been satisfied with his hopes
of success, as well that notwithstanding all his
ambition he was really destitute of courage. At
every step of the narrative henceforth, we can
but mourn that it was Lady Jane Grey's terrible
fate to fall into the power of this man.

In the meantime Mary and her friends exert-
ed themselves to the utmost. In Suffolk, Norfolk, and Cambridgeshire, the great mass of the
people, high-born and low-born, detested the
Duke of Northumberland, and when Mary
pledged herself to make no change in the religion and laws of the land, they in a body
came over to her cause. On the 12th of July
she arrived at Framlingham, and sent to Norwich
to cause her proclamation there. The council
had written her, in reply to her letter, that her
claim to the crown was invalidated by King Edward's will, and by the general voice of the
people. But the council were astonished and

alarmed when news of the disaffection in the counties of Norfolk and Suffolk reached them, and when they also heard that Mary was surrounded by the Earls of Bath and Sussex, Sir Thomas Wharton, Sir John Mordaunt, Sir William Drury, Sir John Shelton, and many other of the nobility and gentry. Northumberland determined upon raising forces immediately to put down the insurrection, as he termed it. But he knew not what to do, for he was the only fit man to head the army, and yet he dared not leave London, for fear that his enemies would in his absence intrigue against him. He concluded to place the Duke of Suffolk at the head of this army, but the queen besought him with tears, and besought the council, that her father might remain with her, and finally determined if necessary to use her authority, and not suffer him to go. There was no other resource left, and Northumberland himself led the army from London. It consisted of six thousand men, well equipped according to the fashion of those times. Before leaving Queen Jane, Northumberland made an appeal to those he left at the Tower, reminding them of their oaths, and telling them that he was willing to put in jeop-

ardy his own life, that her right might be
maintained. "The queen," he said, "by *your*
and *our* enticement, is rather of *force* placed on
the throne, than by her own seeking or request."

Every one present swore to uphold the rights
of Lady Jane, and he proceeded on his way.
But as he was passing through the city he could
not fail to observe the temper of the people,
and he observed to Lord Wilton; "In all this
multitude, my lord, you do not hear one wish
us prosperity!" It was true, and he might have
foreseen, and perhaps did foresee, his own fate
from that hour.

While Lady Jane was at the Tower, on the
12th of July, the Marquis of Winchester delivered to her the crown jewels, gold and silver,
and articles for her wardrobe. The following
were among the things: a "fysshe of gold,
being, a toothpick, a like pendent having one
pearl, and three little pearls at it, a dewberry
of gold, a collet with five pearls, a tablet with a
white and blue sapphire, eight gaurdes of gold
and a tassel of Venice gold, five small agates
with stars graven upon them, a chain with ja-
tinths, table diamonds set in gold, ' etc., etc.

On the 15th of July the commissioners in Flanders wrote to the council as follows:—

"Pleaseth it your good lordships. The four-teenth of this present Don Diego found me, Sir Phillip Hobbye, and me, Sir Richard Morysone, walking in our host's garden, and at his first coming to us entered into a long talk how much he was bound to owe his good will and service to England, and therefore he could not but at one time both sorrow with us for the loss of our good old master, a prince of such virtue and towardness, and also rejoice with us that our master which is departed, did, ere he went, provide us of a king, in regard we had so much cause to rejoice in; he made his excuse that he had come to us the day before, laying the stay thereof in De Arras, for, said he, when I told him I would come to you, and show me a partaker of both your sorrows and gladness, with mind to offer to the king's majesty by you, both of as much service as could lie in me, and of as much as my friends and kinsmen were able to do, in case De Arras did think such my office would not offend the emperor my master; De Arras' advice was that I should for a season defer my going unto you, which as I did somewhat against my will, so I and mine were very glad that so I did, for he telleth me now I may come to you and sorrow with you, and rejoice with you, and make all the offers that I can to the king's majesty, for I shall not only not offend him in so doing, but I shall much please his majesty therewith. And therefore, saith he, do I, and sorrow that you lose so good a king, so do I much rejoice that you have so noble and toward a prince to succeed him, and I promise you, by the words of a gentlemen, I would at all times serve his highness myself and as many as I shall be able to bring with me, if the emperor did call me to serve him. We said we had hitherto received the sorrowful news, but the glad tidings were not as yet come unto us by letters. We were glad to hear this much, and wish we were able to tell him all how things went at home. Saith he, I can tell you this much. The king's majesty, for discharge of his conscience, writ a good piece of his testament with his own hand, barring both his sisters of the crown, and leaving it to the Lady Jane, near to the French queen. Whether the two daughters be bastards or no, or why it is done, we that be strangers have nothing to do

with this matter. Ye are bound to obey and
scrve his majesty, and therefore it is reason we
take him for your king whom the consent of the
nobles of your countrie have declared for your
king, (and saith he) for my part of all others am
bound to be glad that his majesty is set in this
office. I was his god-father, and would as willingly spend my blood in his service as any
subject that he hath, etc., etc."

Two days later the commissioners wrote another communication to the privy council, declaring that they had had an interview with the
emperor, and set forth the substance of the
despatches.

On Sunday, the 16th of July, a sermon was
preached in favor of the new reign at St. Paul's
by Mr. Rogers—a man who, for his boldness,
soon afterwards perished at the stake. That
very day the lord treasurer stole out of the
Tower to his house in London, to make arrangements for the whole council going over to the
cause of Mary. They had until now been in a
manner prisoners, for they dared not leave the
Tower while Northumberland was there. The
news of Mary's advance on London strengthened
the hopes of her adherents there, and rendered

gloomy the partizans of Queen Jane. Fearing that Mary might escape from her castle—which was situated near the German ocean—by sea to the continent, some days before, the govern-ment had sent six ships of war down to the Suf-folk coast, to intercept any vessels containing her ; but these ships, as soon as they arrived at Yarmouth, went over to the side of Mary, and at once added strength to her position. She had now around her an army several thousands strong, and on the 16th all the ships at Harwich declared in her favor. The news of this alarm-ing popularity of Mary's cause could not have failed to carry fear to the heart of the council, and especially the Duke of Suffolk, who was really, in the absence of Northumberland, the head of the government. Letters arrived from Northumberland, demanding immediate rein-forcements, and acknowledging that his army was rapidly deserting him. The council was now fully determined upon making some suita-ble excuse for leaving the Tower, and Lady Jane to her fate. Professing to comply with the demand of Northumberland for more troops, they sent a body of men out of London under the charge of the Earls of Pembroke and Arun-

i

del, who were, as they knew, secretly the friends of Mary. Suffolk was completely deceived, for he prepared the following dispatch to be sent by them :—

"To our trusty and well-beloved Sir John Bridges and Sir Nicholas Poynty, Knights.

"JANE THE QUEEN.

"Trusty and well-beloved, we greet you well, because we doubt not but this our most lawful possession of the crown with the free consent of the nobility of our realm, and other the states of the same, as both plainly known and accepted of you, as our most loving subjects, therefore we do not reiterate the same, but now most earnestly will and require, and by authority hereof warrant you to assemble, muster, and levy, all the power that you can possibly make, either of your servants, tenants, officers, or friends, as well horsemen as footmen, repairing to our right trusty and right well-beloved cousins, the Earls of Arundel and Pembroke, their tenants, servants, and officers, and with the same to repair, with all possible speed, towards Buckinghamshire, for the repression and subduing of certain tumults and rebellions moved there against our

crown by certain seditious men. For the repression whereof we have given orders to divers
others our good subjects, and gentlemen of such
degree as you are, to repair in like manner to
the same parties. So as we nothing doubt but
upon the access of such our loving subjects as
be appointed for that purpose to the place where
the seditious people yet remain, the same shall
either lack heart to abide in their malicious
purpose, or else receive such punishment and
execution as they deserve, seeking the destruction of their native country, and the subversion
of all men in their degrees, by rebellion of the
base multitude, whose rage being stirred, as of
late years hath been seen, must needs be the
confusion of the common weal. Wherefore our
special trust is in your courage, wisdom, and
fidelity in this matter, to advance yourselves
both with power and speed in this enterprise, in
such sort, as by ye the nobility and council shall
also be prescribed unto you. And for the sus-
tentation of your charge in this behalf, by our
said commandment, do further give order to your
satisfaction, as by their letters also shall appear
unto you. And beside that we assure you of
our special consideration of this your service to

us and our crown, as expressly to the preservation of this our realm and commonwealth.
Given under our signet at the Tower of London, on the 18th day of July, the first year
of our reign."

The efforts of Northumberland's party to sus-
tain themselves were made in vain. For the
whole English nation regarded the Duke as a
dangerous and tyrannical man, and also were
convinced that to Mary the throne properly
belonged, and now that she had solemnly promised to make no change in the religion of the
country, they were contented that she should
assume the crown. The privy council was also,
at this very time, in secret devoted to Mary,
and almost the only personage of influence left
at London, who was sincerely devoted to Lady
Jane Grey, was her own father, the Duke of
Suffolk.

Northumberland at Cambridge, though at the
head of an army, made no stand against the
enemy, but endeavored to convince the people
by argument that his daughter-in-law was right-
fully Queen of England. He asked Dr. Landys,
a learned and ardent Protestant, to preach in sup-

port of the claims of Lady Jane, and he did so, attacking with boldness both Mary's character and her title to the throne. In London, Cecil, Cranmer, and the rest of the privy councillors, persuaded Suffolk that it was necessary to raise a large force and put them in their hands, they being just ready to declare for Mary, but carefully disguising their real sentiments.

On the 19th day of July a large portion of the council were at Baynard Castle, the seat of the Earl of Pembroke, just out of London. They had persuaded the Duke of Suffolk that it was necessary for them to leave the Tower, but they were no sooner fairly out of his reach, than they concerted a plan for instantly revolutionizing London. Early in the morning, news reached London from the lord-lieutenant of Essex, that the Earl of Oxford had deserted to the side of Mary, and the following despatch to the lord-lieutenant was sent from the Tower :—

"After our right hearty commendations to your lordships, although the matter contained in your letters of the Earl of Oxford departing to the Lady Mary be grievous unto us for divers respects, yet we must needs give your lordship our hearty thanks for your ready ad·

vertisement thereof. Requiring your lordship nevertheless, like a nobleman, to remain in that promise and steadfastness to our sovereign lady, Queen Jane's service, as ye shall find us ready and firm with all our force to the same. Which neither with honor, nor with safety, nor .yet with duty, we may now forsake.

"From the Tower of London, the 19th of July, 1553."

During the forenoon, while a portion of the council were in the Tower with Lady Jane, another part were assembled in Baynard Castle. The Earl of Arundel at once moved a resolution of allegiance to Queen Mary; Pembroke seconded it, and placing his hand upon his sword, boldly declared that he was ready to dispute the matter with any man who dared oppose the authority of Lady Mary. The whole of the party were unanimous in their support of Mary, and news of the transaction flew to the streets of London. The lord mayor and alder-men were sent for, and Mary was proclaimed in the streets. The people rejoiced, for they were delivered from the rule of the detested Northum-berland. Undoubtedly, however, there were many who grew sorrowful when they thought of the gentle Lady Jane, who had scarcely an enemy in England. The people loved and pitied her, while they rejoiced in the downfall of her father-in-law. The Earl of Arundel and Lord Paget set off instantly to Mary with the important news of the revolution at London. The happiness of the Londoners seemed half-frantic; caps were thrown into the air; the Earl of Pembroke "threwe awaye his cape full of angelles;" money was thrown out of the windows to the crowd by the partisans of Mary; bonfires raged, and bells pealed for joy.

The commotion in the streets soon was known to the inhabitants of the Tower. The Duke of Suffolk was so frightened as to act with the most lamentable lack of manliness. As soon as he heard that Mary was proclaimed in the streets, he came out of the Tower, commanding his partisans to throw aside their weapons, for he was but one man, and himself upon Tower Hill proclaimed the Lady Mary to be the lawful Queen of England! The duke was very much dejected, and went to Lady Jane's apartments and told her that she must lay aside her royalty and all its ceremonies, and advised her to bear her sorrowful fortunes with patience.

In her reply we see the sweet humility which ever dwelt in her heart. She said that her fortitude was greater than he had imagined, and that this summons was more welcome to her than that which raised her to the throne. "In obedience to you, my lord," said she, "and to my mother, I acted violence on myself, and have been guilty of a grievous offence; but the present is my own act, and I willingly resign to correct another's fault, if so great a fault can be corrected by my resignation and sincere acknowledgment."

As soon as Lady Jane had replied thus, she retired to her private apartment, and in solitude pondered on her dangerous situation. Yet, as all the chroniclers of her times agree in declaring, she manifested not the slightest symptom of fear, but wore the same sweet, calm, half-sorrowful countenance, which ever was the brightest charm of her personal appearance.

As soon as Suffolk had deposed Lady Jane, he sent a dispatch to Northumberland, requiring him at once to disband his army, and submit to Queen Mary. But that cowardly though ambitious man, as we shall shortly see, needed no such command to render him willing to give

the crown to Mary. The council decided that
Lady Jane should give up the title of queen—
which she most willingly and joyously had done
several hours before—and all the privileges and
ceremonials attached to the position which she
had innocently usurped. It is said, to illustrate
the suddenness of the revolution in London, that
on the morning of the momentous 19th, Lady
Jane stood god-mother to a child in baptism,
and was attended with all the loyal honors due
to a queen, but in the afternoon she was not
only deposed but virtually a prisoner. At last
the order came from Queen Mary for her arrest
on a charge of high treason, and she was placed
in close confinement. The only thing which
seems to have touched her heart, was the cruel
separation from her husband, Lord Guildford
Dudley. They were both young, handsome,
and undoubtedly loved each other, and their
separation at such a time, and under such
gloomy prospects, must have been heart-rend-
ing. Dudley was not exactly to her that he
was on her marriage-day, for then his heart was
pure, and full of truest love for Lady Jane.
Since that day ambition had once got the better of his love, and though he saw his wife

14

weeping and fainting in her anguish, and re-
fusing to accept the crown, yet he pressed the
bitter cup upon her, and would take no denial.
Yet she loved him, undoubtedly, notwithstanding his cruelty.   But what must have been his
remorse, after this misfortune came, when he
thought of his own agency in the unfortunate
usurpation!

CHAPTER X.

WHEN the news of the revolution in London
reached Northumberland, at Cambridge, he was
struck with terror. Seeing that the people in
the streets were enthusiastic in their joy, he conceived the insane idea that by hurrahing with
them, and joining them in their demonstrations,
he might save his own life. A man of his high
position, who had usurped the crown, should
either have fought to the last against his enemies, or have calmly awaited his dreadful fate
like a man, with dignity and with courage; and
the world would at least have looked upon him
without contempt. But the affrighted man ran
into the market-place, and shouted for Queen
Mary, tossed his cap high in the air and wept,

he pretended, for joy! But the tears were those of fright, of anguish, notwithstanding his pre- tences. Dr. Sandys, the clergyman who only the Sunday before, had preached boldly against Mary, stood by his side. He was a man of real courage and true piety, ready alike for success or for the scaffold. The miserable duke said to him:

"Queen Mary is a merciful woman, and doubt- less all will receive the benefit of her pardon."

"Flatter not yourself," replied Dr. Sandys, "for were the queen ever so much inclined to pardon you, those who rule her will destroy you, whoever else is spared."

Sir John Gates, who had been a tool of Nor- thumberland's, arrested him now, but in the course of a few hours he was set at liberty. When the Earl of Arundel entered the city at the head of a body of troops, he at once arrest- ed Northumberland, Gates, and Dr. Sandys, and committed them to the Tower. Soon after, the Duke and Duchess of Suffolk, the Marquis of Northampton, the Earl of Huntingdon, and others were arrested.

On the 3d of August, Queen Mary arrived at Wanstead, her seat, and disbanded her army,

with the exception of a body of horse. The
Duchess of Suffolk had been liberated after a
few hours' imprisonment, and when she met the
queen she fell upon her knees, and begged
mercy for her husband, the Duke of Suffolk,
saying that he was ill, and would die if shut
up in the Tower. The queen was pleased to
hear her prayer, and liberated the duke. Thus
the couple who had literally forced Lady Jane
into acceptance of the crown were free, while
the innocent victim of their wicked ambition
lay in her dismal place of imprisonment. The
duchess had not a word to say for her gentle
daughter, no pardon to ask, and she did not
hesitate to take part in the public ceremonies of
the occasion! Years afterwards, when Mary
slaughtered the saints with an almost diabolical
perseverance, the Duchess of Suffolk still remained her friend and professed admirer!

In the afternoon of the 3d of August, Queen
Mary entered the city. She rode upon a white
horse, and was dressed in violet velvet, and
looked somewhat fair, though near forty years
of age. Elizabeth rode next after her sister, the
queen. All London was in the streets, and
when the queen arrived at the Tower, she re-

leased many prisoners, who had long been confined there.   The majority of them were Catholics, however.   It soon became evident that Mary
did not intend to fulfil her first promise not to
alter the established religious laws of the country.   A Protestant came up to London with a
petition from his fellow-believers, and was put
in the pillory! This was the prelude to those
terrible acts which will ever be associated with
the name of Queen Mary.

About this time letters were received from
the commissioners in Flanders, revealing the
singular fact that the despatches which were
received from them by Northumberland some
time previous, were devoid of truth, and intended to deceive, for from the first the emperor
had expressed himself utterly opposed to Lady
Jane's usurpation of the throne!

On the 18th of August, the Duke of Northumberland had his trial.   He acted towards his
judges with great humility.   It is not a little
singular that among his judges were men who
had acted with him as councillors to Lady Jane
Grey!   He said to the judges that he spoke not
anything in defence of himself, yet he wished
the opinion of the court on two points: First,

whether a man, acting by authority of the prince and council, and by warrant of the great seal of England, might properly be charged of treason.

Secondly, whether any of the persons who acted with him, and of course were equally guilty, might be his judges, or pass upon his trial at his death!

The reply of the court was that the seal he used was not the seal of the lawful queen, but the seal of an usurper, and secondly, that any persons who were not attainted of treason, could with the pleasure of the queen, sit upon the tial The duke saw that words would avail him nothing, and confessed his crimes and begged their pardon. Throughout the trial he conducted himself in the basest manner possible. There is one exception; for he assured the court what ever might be his own deserts, that Lady Jane not only did not aspire to the crown, but was *by enticement and force* made to accept of it. This was the only generous sentiment which fell from the lips of the duke during his trial. For himself, he craved the death which was usually accorded to noblemen, and beseeched that his children might be treated favorably. He also wished to confer with some eminent divine upon religious matters. He hoped still to save his life by renouncing his Protestantism.

The rejoicing of the people was great when they heard of the sentence of condemnation against the Duke of Northumberland. They felt that at last justice had overtaken him for his despotic acts. When he was carried back from the court to his prison in the Tower, a woman, probably alluding to the execution of Somerset by Northumberland, saluted him with the words, "Behold the blood which thou didst cause to be unjustly shed does now apparently begin to revenge itself on thee!"

On the 19th of August, Northumberland received news that it was the intention of the government to proceed at once to his execution, and he immediately wrote the following letter to the Earl of Arundel:

"Honorable lord, and in this my distress my especial refuge, most woful was the news I received this evening by Mr. Lieutenant, that I must prepare myself against to-morrow to receive the deadly stroke. Alas, my good lord, is my crime so heinous as no redemption but my blood can

wash away the spots thereof? An old proverb
there is, and that most true, that a living dog is
better than a dead lion. Oh! that it would
please her good grace to give me life, yea the
life of a dog, if I might but live and kiss her
feet, and spend both life and all in her honorable service, as I have the best part already under
her worthy and most glorious father. Oh! that
her mercy were such as she would consider
how little profit my dead and dismembered
body can bring her, but how great and glorious
an honor it will be in all posterities when the
report shall be, that so gracious and mighty a
queen had granted life to so miserable and
penitent an object. Your honorable usage and
promise to me since these my troubles, have
made me bold to challenge this kindness at your
hands. Pardon me, if I have done amiss therein,
and spare not, I pray, your bended knees for
me in this distress. The God of heaven it may
be will requite one day on you or yours. And
if my life be lengthened by your mediation and
my good lord chancellors, (to whom I have also
sent my blurred letters,) I will ever owe it to be
spent at your honorable feet. Oh! good my lord,
remember how sweet life is, and how bitter the
J

contrary. Spare not your speech and pains, for God, I hope, hath not shut out all hopes of comfort from me in that gracious, princely, and woman-like heart; but that as the doleful news of death hath wounded to death both my soul and body, so a comfortable news of life shall be as a new resurrection to my woful heart. But if no remedy can be found, either by imprisonment, confiscation, banishment, and the like, I can say no more, but God grant me the patience to endure, and the heart to forgive the whole world.

"Once your fellow and loving companion, but now worthy of no name but wretchedness and misery.   J. D."

This letter shows very clearly the real character of Northumberland. Although a man of iron nerve and most reckless disposition, yet in view of death his courage all vanishes, and he cries in his agony like a child, for help. How strangely does the conduct of Lady Jane contrast with his own at this crisis! She, though young and gentle, has not a word of complaint, not a single thrill of fear; but the old, weather-beaten soldier begs most shamefully for "yea, the life of a dog!"

But the base supplication was fruitless, for on the 22d day of August, the lieutenant of the Tower delivered to the sheriffs of London the Duke of Northumberland, Sir John Gates, and Sir Thomas Palmer, for execution. When the duke and Sir John Gates met, the former said:

"Sir John, God have mercy upon us, for this day shall end both our lives, and I pray you forgive me whatsoever I have offended, and I forgive you with all my heart, although you and your council were a great occasion thereof."

Sir John replied:

"Well, my lord, I forgive you all, as I would be forgiven, and yet you and your authority were the original cause of it altogether, but the Lord pardon you, and I pray you forgive me."

The duke laid aside his gown, and leaning upon the railing, made an address to the multitude of people congregated to witness his execution. The day before he heard mass in his prison, and boldly avowed himself a Catholic, thus deserting his old creed. He confessed that he was worthy of death; that he had helped in the false religion, and for this God had punished the nation by the death of Henry VIII., Edward VI.; with rebellion, and with sweating

sickness. He was thankful that now he was a
Christian, though for sixteen years he had not
been one. He guarded his hearers against cove-
tousness, which was the cause of his fate, and
said, "I beseech you all to bear me witness that
I die in the true Catholic faith." He then repeated several Latin psalms, and afterwards said:
"Into thy hands, O Lord, I commend my spirit," and bending toward the block, said that he
deserved a thousand deaths; when his neck
lay upon it, it was instantly severed. Gates
and Palmer were immediately after executed.
Thus perished the man who was the cause of
so much intense suffering to innocent persons,
through his inordinate ambition.

But it is time that we return to Lady Jane
Grey and her unfortunate husband. They were
now state-prisoners, and confined in separate
apartments. Beauchamp's Tower was the general place of confinement for state-prisoners, but
Lady Jane was imprisoned in one of the warden's houses, inside of the prison walls, kept by
a "Master Partridges." It is probable that
her comfort was better secured in the warden's
house than it could have been in the usual
prison apartments. She was allowed to retain

two of her female attendants, but the day after she became a prisoner, the Marquis of Winchester, the lord treasurer, required of her to deliver up the crown jewels, or those which were in her possession. The sympathy of the nation for Lady Jane was unquestionable, unmistakable. Northumberland was hated; but for his lovely and innocent victim there was nothing but pity, save in the hearts of a few heartless courtiers, or bigoted and fierce Catholics. The nation loved as its own existence the principle of hereditary right, and never could quietly consent to see Mary defrauded of her throne, yet it blamed not the pious and gentle-hearted Lady Jane Grey for her agency in the unfortunate usurpation. A feeling of sympathy for her, and even for her husband in a lesser degree, filled the hearts of the people, and it was generally hoped that no punishment would be inflicted upon them. The Duke and Duchess of Suffolk, though a hundred times more guilty than Lady Jane, had been set free, why should not the victim of their advice and commands also receive her liberty!

The conduct of Lady Jane upon her imprisonment will, as long as the history of England

and the Reformation is remembered, place her
name upon the scroll of heroes and martyrs who
perished bravely and gloriously. History fur-
nishes no instance where a girl of sixteen con-
ducts herself through trial, imprisonment, and
death with greater courage, mildness, and resignation than were exhibited by Lady Jane Grey.

She was young, and loved life and liberty;
she was full of the warmest affections; yet she
parted from the fair husband in whose bosom
she had lain, without a murmur, and laid off the
habiliments of a queen for a prison-life, without
a sigh! Her conduct during this change was
truly remarkable. Fuller says that "she made
misery itself amiable by her pious and patient
behavior; adversity, her night clothes, bearing
her, as well as her day-dressing, by reason of
her pious disposition."

Burnet says, "she was so humble, so gentle,
and pious, that all people both admired and
loved her. That she had a mind wonderfully
raised above the world, and at the age wherein
others are but imbibing the notions of philosophy, she had attained to the practice of the
highest precepts of it: for she was neither lifted
up with the hope of a crown, nor cast down

when she saw her palace made afterwards her prison; but carried herself with an equal temper of mind in the great inequalities of fortune that so suddenly exalted and depressed her."

Through all her long imprisonment this angelic creature never uttered a complaint of her suffering, and seemed to be wholly concerned for her father and husband, who had forced her to act the part which she did, and which must be expiated by the sacrifice of her life. When London was alive with enthusiasm upon the advent of Mary, Lady Jane was alone in her apartment, and listened to the booming of the cannon and the shouts of the populace in silence. It is not strange that her pious heart soon came to the conclusion that this world of bitter disappointment was nothing in comparison to that glorious world towards which her meek spirit was hastening. Queen Mary entered the Tower and liberated many prisoners there, but she came not to "Master Partridge's" house, where was the young Lady Jane, her cousin.

Before the coronation of Queen Mary, she issued an order to the lord treasurer which commenced as follows:

"BY THE QUEEN.

"Mary the Queen.

"Trusty and well beloved, we greet you well. And where upon delivery of certain of our jewels and stuff to your hands by the Lady Jane Grey, the 20th of July last, which she had before received of you the 12th of the same month, it appeareth that the parcels hereafter mentioned were wanting, and by occasion thereof cannot be found again; forasmuch as we certainly understood that by your diligence all the rest that she had was recovered, being at the same time in like danger, and upon trust we have ye will not let to use the like travel to recover those parcels to our use as soon as ye can," etc., etc. There follows a list of the lost articles—lost probably in the agitation and confusion attendant upon the suddenness of the change of Lady Jane's condition. It seems that every penny in the possession of Lady Jane or her husband, Guildford Dudley, was taken from them, as if in part to make up to loss of certain articles of state.

At the time of Northumberland's death the imperial ambassadors urged Queen Mary to bring Lady Jane to trial; but she seems not to have been willing, either because her heart would not allow of it, or she feared to outrage the feelings of the people too far. It is said that she declared that she had no heart to put to death her unfortunate cousin, whom she regarded as the victim of Northumberland. About this time Lady Jane addressed a narrative of her term of royalty, to Queen Mary, in which she confessed her fault, but declared that when Northumberland and her father and mother came to her, and attempted to force the crown upon her, that she fell to the ground fainting, as one dead, and remained their helpless victim. The cause of this address to the queen was not to intercede for her own life or that of Dudley, but to show her majesty the innocence of herself in the transaction. Lady Jane was pious and good, and loved a good reputation better than life, and wished Queen Mary to know that she had not acted with wilful wickedness in the usurpation, but had been forced to act the part allotted to her. Whether the true statement of the case had any effect upon the queen we know not, but the conduct of her officers towards Lady Jane was harsh in the extreme. The charge that some of the crown jewels were lost

j   15

was merely a pretence, and under it Lady Jane
and Dudley were literally robbed of their private jewels, and all the money in their possession. There is a meanness in such an act almost
without a parallel in history. For a proud
Queen of England to seize upon the pocket-
money of an unfortunate woman, who was niece
to a king, certainly was the lowest depths of
niggardliness.

The Sunday after the execution of Northumberland, the old Catholic service was chanted
in St. Paul's, and on every hand it soon became
apparent that Mary would soon commence a
career of persecution. Throughout the month
of August, sharp struggles took place between
the Catholics and Protestants, for the possession
of the churches, and the government seemed to
be undecided whether boldly to proclaim Catholicism in opposition to the principles of the Reformation. All doubts were soon dispersed, however, by the course pursued by the ministry. Mary
was desirous of placing the Pope at the head of
the church, but even her Catholic bishop, Gardiner, opposed this scheme. Her answer to him
is a memorable one.

" Women, I have read in Scripture, are

forbidden to speak in church. Is it then fit-
ting that *your* church should have a dumb
head?"

On the 15th of September, Archbishop Cranmer, Latimer, and others, were arrested and
committed to prison. All doubt was at an end
now,—Queen Mary was determined to distin-
guish herself as a heretic-burner; a religious
persecutor.

During the last week in September, the queen
was busily occupied in preparing for her approaching coronation. She had no money left
in her treasury, and was obliged to borrow
£20,000 of the citizens of London for the occasion. The day appointed was the first of October. Three days before the coronation, the queen
set out from Whitehall by barge for the Tower,
attended by the lord mayor and different honorable companies. At the Tower, she made fifteen knights of the bath, and remaining over
night, the next day she went in grand procession
through the streets of London.

On the coronation morning, the queen and
her numerous attendants took their barges, and
proceeded to the stairs leading to Parliament-
chamber. The whole city was in the streets,

notwithstanding the day before had been one of
the utmost pomp and pageantry. The Parlia-
ment-chamber was splendidly hung with tapes-
try, and blue cloth was laid in the street, from
Parliament-hall to Westminster Abbey. At
about ten o'clock the queen was conducted to
the robing-chamber, where she waited till eleven,
when the procession commenced to the Abbey.
Bishop Gardiner performed the part usually allotted to the Archbishop of Canterbury, pro-
nouncing the coronation-oaths. Mary was attired in royal robes of velvet, a mantle with a
train, a surcoat, a riband of Venice gold, a mantle-lace of gold and silk, with buttons and tassels
of the same material, having the imperial crown
on her head, the sceptre in her right hand, an
orb in her left, and a pair of gold-crimson seba-
tons on her feet. Mary's personal appearance at
this time was not striking. Nearly forty years
old, low in stature, very thin and pale in her face,
which was not indicative of either intellect or
good nature, she made little impression through
her beauty, though she was by no means re-
pulsive in her appearance. After the principal
ceremonies were over, a general pardon of prisoners was read, but it contained so many excep-

tions, that to many the day was a day of sorrow rather than a day of rejoicing.

When the queen left Westminster Abbey it was in a robe of purple velvet, an open surcoat of the same material, with miniver and powdered ermine, a mantle-lace of silk and gold, a riband of gold, and a crown upon her head. The banquet followed, and among the entertainments of the occasion were dramatic and comic representations. The comedian, Heywood, presented himself at court, from banishment. The queen asked him:

"What wind has blown you hither?"

"Two special ones," said Heywood, "one of them to see your majesty."

"We thank you for that," replied Mary, "but I pray for what purpose was the other?"

"That your majesty might see *me!*" replied the comedian.

His wit was successful, and the queen often saw him, and amused herself with his comic representations.

During all this pageantry Lady Jane Grey remained in her prison, separated from her husband and all her friends; yet she was happy,

for she had the peace "which passeth all understanding."

In a few days Mary's first parliament was
opened. Its first act was to repeal all former
acts of Henry VIII.'s reign in reference to
Katharine of Arragon and her daughter, Queen
Mary. Its next was to pass a bill of attainder
upon Lady Jane Grey and her husband.

CHAPTER XI.

THE trial of Lady Jane Grey and her husband, Lord Guildford Dudley, on a charge of
high treason, took place at the Guildhall on the
13th of November. Archbishop Cranmer, Lord
Ambrose and Sir Henry Dudley, were at this
time also charged with treason. The time of
Lady Jane's trial was in the saddest month of
the English year—a month usually crowded full
of sombre skies and melancholy fogs. On the
morning of the memorable 13th of November, a
morning, probably, like almost all November
days in London, overcast with the solemnest
clouds of autumn, Lady Jane and Lord Guildford were led from the Tower, in which so long

they had been incarcerated, to Guildhall, to take their trial.. They were surrounded by a guard of four hundred halberdiers, and great noise and confusion were attendant upon the procession to the place of trial, yet Lady Jane bore herself with courage and calmness. From the day on which she was imprisoned to this day she had not seen her husband, but this morning they met. We can easily imagine what a sad meeting it must have been, and how eagerly each scanned the face of the other to discover with what patience and Christian meekness the imprisonment had been borne. When the unfortunate pair entered the court-room, there was present a great crowd of witnesses, and the ceremonies which characterized the trial were exceedingly impressive. But Lady Jane was, throughout the whole scene, perfectly calm and seemingly happy. Her judges were men well calculated to intimidate a young and tender woman, but she was not agitated in the least. Her cheeks were blooming all the while, and her voice trembled not, nor in any manner did she show fear or agitation. To the charge against her Lady Jane pleaded guilty, though she was most innocently so, and guiltless of any

intention to rob another of her rights.   The
sentence was pronounced by Lord Chief Justice
Morgan, and a most terrible one it was.   She
was sentenced to be burnt alive on Tower Hill
or beheaded, at the queen's pleasure.   When
this dreadful sentence was pronounced, a groan
burst forth from almost every person present,
and when Lady Jane set out on her return to
the Tower, great crowds of people followed
her, crying aloud, and bewailing her fate.   The
sympathy for her was exceedingly great, and
she was obliged to offer consolation to those
who followed her.   Turning to them she said,
with angelic sweetness,

"Oh! faithful companions of my sorrows,
why do you thus afflict me with your plaints?
Are we not born into life to suffer adversity,
and even disgrace, if it be necessary?   When
has the time been that the innocent were not
exposed to violence and oppression?"

We must remember that all this sympathy
was shown for Lady Jane when a universal
opinion obtained that she was to be pardoned
by Queen Mary.   How much more powerful it
would have been in view of her death, we can
readily imagine.   The queen, notwithstanding

her hardness of heart, was touched with pity for Lady Jane, when she beheld her meek and gentle conduct. There is not the slightest reason to doubt her intention at this time to pardon Lady Jane and her husband, Lord Guildford Dudley. She ordered that the former be allowed the liberty of walking in the queen's garden at the Tower, and on the hill. Lord Guildford also received a gentler treatment than before, having the liberties of the "ports" where he was lodged. On the 21st of December, the Marquis of Northampton and Sir Henry Gates were both pardoned and released from prison, and immediately Lady Jane Grey and Lord Dudley experienced a change in their treatment, which must have led them to believe that soon the queen would set them at liberty. Alas! that the mad and foolish acts of others, who were already free from the miseries of a prison life, should bear such a sad sway over their fortunes!

Queen Mary showed an intense desire to win Lady Jane over to the Catholic faith, and learned papist divines were sent to argue with her, and endeavor to show her the wickedness of the doctrines of the Reformation. We have no doubt but Mary really longed to see Lady Jane a good Catholic, and from the best of motives. She was cruel and persecuting, not because she loved blood, but because she was ignorantly, bigotedly, madly devoted to the Catholic religion. But it was utterly useless to attempt to shake Lady Jane in her belief. As an old writer remarks, "all their labors were bootless, for she had art to confound their art, wisdom to withstand their flatteries, resolution above their menaces, and such a true knowledge of life, that death was to her no other than a most familiar acquaintance."

A convocation of the clergy previous to this had declared the Book of Common Prayer to be an abomination, and also demanded a supervision of the Catechism, and recommended immediate persecution against all of the clergy who did not put away their wives, and adopt the Catholic article of belief in reference to the real presence. The whole influence of the government was in favor of the Catholic religion, and in those days, when the scaffold and the stake were commonly used to terrify the people into compliance with the wishes of the court, the influence of the government was exceedingly powerful. The truth was, that many of those who, under the reign of Edward VI., had called themselves Protestants, were so merely because it was for their personal interest to be so, and the moment that a Catholic occupied the throne, they retreated back at once into the bosom of the Romish church. A majority of the clergy became Catholic, and some of the bishops; but Cranmer and Latimer were sent to the Tower, and soon after the Archbishop of York for marrying, and Ridley for preaching at St. Paul's in favor of Lady Jane's usurpation, Poynet for marriage, and several other of the bishops for similar offences, were sentenced to imprisonment. Dr. Sandys, who so boldly, at Cambridge, preached against the title of Mary to the throne, though at first imprisoned, was afterwards liberated by the queen. One of the ladies of her bedchamber interceded for the bold and honest preacher, and one day when Gardiner came to the privy chamber the queen said:

"Winchester, what think you about Dr. Sandys? Is he not sufficiently punished?"

"As it pleases your majesty," answered the bishop.

"Then, truly," replied Queen Mary, "we

would have him set at liberty." She signed immediately the warrant for his releasement, and he was set free. The friends of Queen Mary attempt, from such acts as these, to rescue her name from the opprobrium which has covered it for centuries, and we think they certainly show that she was not wholly lost to tender emotions. But it is impossible to forget the many terrible acts for which Queen Mary ever must be held responsible by just men, and which shroud her memory in a pall of darkness. Undoubtedly her ministers were constantly pressing her on in her career of persecution, but a true Queen of England should have been superior to her cabinet, and have guided them, instead of being contented to be led *by* them.

About this time certain of the inhabitants of the county of Suffolk reminded the queen that she solemnly promised them before her coronation that she would not change the reformed religion as it was established under her brother, Edward VI. But the queen did not like thus to be reminded of her broken promises, and one man, who was bolder than his companions in complaining, was put in the pillory. Judge

Hales, a Protestant, who had refused to countenance Lady Jane Grey's usurpation, simply
because of his strict honesty of character, was
thrust into a loathsome dungeon, where he soon
grew crazy and endeavored to make way with
his life.   At last he was liberated, but his health
and mind were ruined.

Mary now determined upon marriage, to make
sure of a Catholic succession. All her life she
had been trying to marry, and now there was an
eligible opportunity to wed the son of the Emperor Charles, to whom (the father) she had
been thirty years before engaged.   It is said
that Mary really loved Edward Courtenay, Earl
of Devon, whom she had liberated from prison,
a handsome and exceedingly accomplished gentleman.   But unfortunately he was suspected of
sympathizing with the Protestants, and regarded
the Princess Elizabeth with more affection than
Queen Mary. The queen also had some thoughts
of wedding the celebrated Cardinal Pole, who
had never taken priest's orders.   The main
reason for dismissing this project, was the advanced age of the cardinal, he being now fifty-
three years old.

The Emperor Charles sent over his ambassa-

dors for the purpose of arranging a marriage
between his son Philip and the English Queen.
They had constant access to her, and she, without even asking the advice of her council, made
a solemn engagement of herself to Philip.

For a short time the engagement was kept a
secret, but when it came out, the whole country
was filled with discontent. The English people
feared that with a Spanish prince for the husband of their queen, England would sink into a
state of vassalage to Spain. Many Catholics
opposed the marriage, and the entire Protestant
body were bitterly against it. They boldly declared that Mary's sole object was " to continue
Popery where it was, and to bring it in where it
was not." The speaker and twenty members
of Parliament petitioned her majesty that she
would not marry a stranger or a foreigner. The
queen thought that Gardiner, her favorite bishop, originated this movement, and said she
would prove a match for his cunning. That
very evening she sent for the Spanish ambassador, and leading him into her private oratory,
she knelt before the altar, and after she had
repeated the hymn *Veni Creator*, she called
upon God to witness that while she lived she

would never marry any man but Philip of
Spain.

In December, Parliament was dissolved, to
get rid of a troublesome enemy. In January,
Count Egmont arrived from Spain, to conclude
the marriage-treaty. There were at once tokens
of revolt, for the people of Kent, where the
count landed, rose in large masses and endeavored to obtain his person. He arrived at London safely, and the marriage-treaty was arranged.
The terms were as follows: Philip was to have
the honor of the title of King of England, but the
government was to rest solely with the queen,
he merely aiding her in her duties. No Span-
iard was to enjoy any of the offices of the kingdom; no innovations were to be made in the laws
and customs of England; the queen was never to
be carried abroad without her free consent, nor
any of her children, if she had any, without the
consent of the nobility. Philip, in case Mary survived him, was to settle upon her a jointure of
£60,000 a year; the male issue of the marriage
was to inherit Burgundy and the Low Countries,
as well as England; and in case Don Carlos, Philip's son by his first marriage, were to die and
leave no issue, then their issue, whether male or

female, were to inherit Spain, Sicily, and Milan.
The treaty was concluded, but notwithstanding
the concessions made by the Spanish prince, the
English people were dissatisfied. In less than
a week Queen Mary and her court were alarmed
by the intelligence that Sir Peter Carew was up
in arms in Devonshire, to resist the advent of
Philip of Spain, and that already he had taken
possession of the city and castle of Exeter.
News shortly followed to the effect that the
Duke of Suffolk, with his brothers, Lord John
and Lord Leonard Grey, had organized a rebellion in the mid-counties, for the restoration of
the innocent Lady Jane Grey, who seems to
have been the victim of any ambitious and
reckless man in the kingdom. But the most
formidable insurrection was that headed by Sir
Thomas Wyatt. He was only twenty-three
years old, a Catholic, son to an illustrious poet,
full of enthusiasm, and was roused to a high
pitch of excitement in reference to the Spanish
marriage. Thus there were three distinct insurrections in the kingdom, though they were
one in reference to one point—the queen's mar
riage. Sir Peter Carew aimed at placing Elizabeth and the Earl of Devonshire on the throne;

K

16

Wyatt only wished to prevent the foregin marriage; and the Greys looked for the restoration of Lady Jane Grey to the throne. The last personages were the maddest of all. The Duke of Suffolk had once been pardoned for treason ; he was perfectly well aware that there was a good prospect that his daughter would soon be released from her confinement; he also knew that, in case of his success, Lady Jane would never accept of the throne, unless by force she were compelled to do so; we can therefore account for his conduct only upon the ground that he lacked the qualities of mind which men generally possess. A more reckless, foolish, mad, cruel course of conduct he could not have pursued. He passed through Leicestershire, proclaiming Lady Jane Grey in every town through which he journeyed, and, weak man, seemed to sincerely believe that the nation which only a few months before had utterly refused to support his cause, would now rally unitedly around him !

The Earl of Huntingdon, at the head of an army, soon conquered the Grey party, they flying for their lives into distant towns. The duke and his brothers were, however, shortly

afterwards arrested, and imprisoned in the Tower. Sir Peter Carew was also soon put to flight,
he absconding to France.

Wyatt alone remained in the field. He made
a stand at the head of 15,000 men. The queen
sent the Duke of Norfolk with a body of men
against him, at Rochester. There five hundred
soldiers, under the duke, deserted to the side of
Wyatt, and the queen's artillery also fell into
the hands of the insurgents. The Duke of
Norfolk fled, and three-fourths of his troops
went over to Wyatt's side. When the news
arrived at court of this defeat, all London was
in uproar and confusion. If Wyatt had forced
a march upon the capitol, he might, perhaps,
have won a victory over the queen, for she was
almost defenceless; but he was three days in arriving at Greenwich. The queen rode into London, to encourage the citizens by her presence,
and the lord mayor received her at the Guildhall. She there made a speech to the people,
full of mettle and true courage. At the conclusion the populace vociferated loudly, " God save
Queen Mary and the prince of Spain ! " From
Guildhall the queen proceede l to Westminster,
where she held a council, to devise means for

defence. An armed watch was set in White-hall. But at two in the morning the palace was alarmed by news brought by a deserter that Wyatt would be at Hyde Park Corner in two hours! The palace was filled with lamentations and cries of fear; hurried arrangements for defence were made; the people barricaded the streets; and the queen's chamber windows were well guarded, as well as all her apartments. Every woman at court was alarmed, with the exception of Queen Mary, who was calm and fearless. Bishop Gardiner tried to persuade her to take a boat and retreat from the city, but she answered:

"I will set no example of cowardice!"

At four in the morning the drums began to beat to arms, and the queen's forces were so disposed as best to defend Whitehall or the approaches to it. Wyatt's men already were in Kent street, where the people gave them good cheer. They were commanded to refrain from pillage, but could not be restrained from sacking the residence of Bishop Gardiner. His books were cut in pieces, so that, as an old writer says, "men might have gone up to their knees in leaves of books, cut out and thrown under foot."

The morning was a chill, wintry, gloomy one, for it was the 7th of February. It was nine o'clock before Wyatt began fairly to enter the city. He divided his forces into three parts.

The queen's forces were under the leadership of Clinton and Pembroke, and quietly at their posts, awaited the attack from the insurgents. Thousands of the people were gathered to witness the battle, or more properly, petty series of skirmishes. It had been promised Wyatt that Ludgate should be opened for him by the people of that section of the city, and he hastened there with a small force. At the same time two of his leaders—Knevet and Cobham—attacked Whitehall and St. James'. St. James' was well defended by Sir Henry Jermingham, but Whitehall, where the queen was, was in great danger. The guards, commanded by Sir John Gage, gave way before the insurgents. At the time the queen stood in a gallery of the palace, and witnessed the conflict. The defeated soldiers secreted themselves in some of the houses around the palace, and the porter shut the palace gates, so that friends and foes alike were shut out. The soldiers belonging to the queen's standard desired that the gates might be opened to them, and Mary, with excellent courage, ordered that they be immediately opened, and the guards marched in before her. She spoke to them a few words of encouragement, and commanded them not to leave the spot.

Wyatt now fought his way down the Strand towards Ludgate. This street, now the busiest thoroughfare in London, was filled with troops, under Courtenay, Earl of Devonshire. The moment Wyatt appeared, he fled, some suppose from fear, but there is no doubt but that he was a secret ally of Wyatt. The insurgent leader then demanded the warden of Ludgate to surrender. He supposed the warden was a friend, but such was not the case. The commander, Lord Howard, appeared and answered to the summons:

"Avaunt, traitor!—you enter not here!"

Wyatt now was obliged to fight his way back to his main army. In the mean time Courtenay came in hot haste to the queen, saying, "The battle is broke—all is lost!" Mary's spirit was roused, and she replied:

"Such is the fond opinion of those who dare not go near enough to see the truth of the trial. We will go ourself to the battle immediately, and abide the upshot of our rightful quarrel, or die with the brave men fighting for us."

She then prepared herself for the street. At that moment the palace was assaulted in the rear by a body of men under Cobham. A band of gentlemen-at-arms defended the palace with great courage, in the rear, and other men fought well in front with battle-axes. Cries were constantly heard throughout the palace, that all was lost, and the queen was beseeched to make an attempt to escape in a barge down the Thames. But she would not, but was cheerful, and endeavored to impart courage to those around her. She asked:

" Where is Lord Pembroke? "

The answer was:

" He is in the midst of the battle."

" Well, then," said she, " all that dare not fight may fall to prayers, and I warrant we shall hear better news anon. God will not deceive me, in whom my chief trust is."

Still there was the wildest confusion in the palace, and few hearts there were calm. Shrieks were uttered in every room, cheeks were white with fear, but Queen Mary privately left the palace, to cheer the soldiers. She saw that her fate would be decided in a few moments; that she would soon meet with an ignominious end, or at least a terrible disgrace, or she would triumph over her enemies, and stand the proudest queen of the world! She stood between two of her soldiers, within shot of the enemy, and saw the valiant Pembroke make his final charge which decided the battle. Wyatt's forces fled in confusion, and such was the excitement and terror of every one, that friends were mistaken for foes, and the insurgents were only known by their dress, which had been muddied in coming hastily up to London.

Sir Thomas Wyatt sat down upon a stall in Fleet Street, dispirited and fatigued, and in a short time gave himself up quietly a prisoner, and he was carried in triumph to court.

Thus ended the three insurrections, the last one of which came so near being successful, that the court was striken with terror. Alas! the consequence was that the innocent Lady Jane Grey. who had rested unconscious of the battles outside her prison walls, must lay down her life. Her father had not only ensured his own downfall, but that of his daughter. Mary might have rested content with his blood, had there been no insurrection but the feeble one of which he was the head; but Wyatt's frightful approach to success so alarmed her, that she was fully ready to sacrifice whoever, in the opinion of her council, was an enemy to the crown.

CHAPTER XII.

THE rebellion, the details of which we have
just contemplated, was, as we have remarked,
the immediate cause of Lady Jane Grey's death.
Queen Mary was at once beset by her courtiers
and councillors, who persuaded her to believe
that the death of Lady Jane was necessary to
the security of the crown. Alarmed as she had
been by the insurrections, she needed but little
argument to convince her that her innocent relation must be sacrificed. It is a most singular
fact, that the men who were the most urgent in
their desire for Lady Jane's execution, were the
very persons who had forced the crown upon
her, but who by base recantation now stood

high at Mary's court. The Earl of Pembroke
and the Marquis of Westminster were these
men. They had, months before, urged with
the utmost eloquence Lady Jane to accept the
crown; had, when she wept and fainted at the
thought of usurpation, actually pressed the bitter cup to her lips, and now, with a cruelty and
wickedness scarcely surpassed in history com-
passed her death, urged Queen Mary to execute
her at once!

The Duke of Suffolk, Lady Jane's father, was
now, of course, a traitor, and sure of death. His
conduct was characterized by the utmost recklessness, weakness, and madness. Queen Mary
had, with singular good-nature, pardoned him
for his former offence against her, pardoned him
after an imprisonment of only a few days, and
with a miserable grace now came his mad efforts
to raise a rebellion against his benefactor. The
most sad result of his conduct was the effect
which it had upon the fortunes of Lady Jane
Grey. He alone should have borne the penalties
for his misconduct, but in fact the heaviest blow
fell upon Lady Jane Grey, who was made responsible for her father's conduct. The very
next day after the fray with Wyatt, the queen

came to Temple Bar, and upon the spot still
damp with blood, signed the death-warrant of
Lady Jane Grey and Lord Guildford Dudley.
Her excuse was, that as long as a competitor to
the throne existed there would be rebellions, and
the safety of the kingdom demanded the death
of Lady Jane.   The warrant commanded the
execution of the unfortunate pair upon the ninth
day of February—it now being the seventh.
The queen evidently was frightened for her
safety, and not possessing a tender heart, consented to the death of her lovely cousin without
manifesting much feeling. Excuse the act as historians may, it was a frightful one, and it will forever stamp the character of Queen Mary as vindictive, cruel, and bloody. She knew perfectly
well the true history of Lady Jane's usurpation
of the crown—knew of her repugnance at accepting it, of her innocence, her youth, and her
gentle piety—must have known that under no
circumstances could she ever again be persuaded
to accept the crown, and yet, though she was
her relative, yet Mary consigned her, young,
beautiful, and pious as she was, to the scaffold !
Had the queen possessed a woman's heart, she
never would have signed the death-warrant of

Lady Jane Grey. The truth is, her heart was cold, and her affections were withered by repeated disappointments, and she felt but little sympathy for an enemy, in however distressing a condition.

Only two days were allowed to Lady Jane to prepare for her execution, but so full of piety was her heart, that when Feckenham, a Catholic priest, came to announce to her her fate, she declared that she was ready and willing to die! Dr. Feckenham was a bigoted, though a very sincere, and we believe a pious Catholic. He attempted to reason with her upon religious matters, but Lady Jane told him her time was too short for controversy. He at once flew to the queen, and told her that the time was too short for the preparation of Lady Jane for death, and that there could be no hope of winning her over to the true faith so suddenly. The queen therefore respited the execution for three days. Feckenham went immediately to the prison where Lady Jane was, and with his face glowing with pleasure, informed her of the respite. Lady Jane smiled sadly upon him, and replied:

"You have mistaken my meaning; I wish not for delay of sentence, but for quiet from

polemic disputation." The priest seemed surprised, but she went on to make the exquisitely beautiful remark:

"I am prepared to receive patiently my death,
in any manner it may please the queen to appoint. True it is, my flesh shudders, as is natural to frail mortality, but my spirit will spring
rejoicingly into eternal light, where I hope the
mercy of God will receive it!"

From this meek and beautiful reply, we may
judge of the state of Lady Jane's mind. She
was calm, quiet, and fully prepared to die. At
times her spirit seems to have been joyous, at
others, burdened with a sweet melancholy, but
at no time she looked forward to her fate with
horror or bitter regret. Had she indulged in
paroxysms of grief, her conduct would not have
surprised the world, for she was very young and
frail, but her sublime courage won the sympathy of all hearts.

Queen Mary was enraged at her calm reply
to Feckenham, and determined, if possible, to
force the truth upon her—to persecute her in
her few last hours, by wearisome religious disputes. She sent Feckenham again to her, and
also sent several able Catholic divines, to discuss

with her the truths of the Catholic belief. Feck
enham had little doubt but with the fear of
death before her eyes, he should have an easy
victory over his friend, Lady Jane, and begged
of her to appoint an hour for the discussion of
matters, which he insisted upon so deeply affected her eternal welfare. She beseeched of him,
in reply, if he really had any compassion for
her, to leave her to herself, to commune in solemn silence with her Maker, before whose throne
she hoped soon to appear. To this gentle creature, whose death was certain to occur in a few
hours, the prospect of a polemic discussion with
a wily, though undoubtedly pious priest, must
have been painful. She needed her few last
hours for prayer and quiet contemplation, and
it would be strange if, in sight of the scaffold, a
young girl were to prove a match for a calm
and learned priest, in disputation. But Feckenham was bent upon a display of his powers,
and Lady Jane consented to the discussion. To
make the matter worse, Feckenham invited in a
number of the clergy and others to witness the
dispute. Among the witnesses were the noble
and learned, who came to see a professed disputant vanquish a girl in religious argument.

That scene would make a remarkable subject for an artist. It was within the walls of the bloody Tower, between a sombre, learned, bigoted priest on the one side, and a fair, blooming, lovely girl on the other; and a crowd of witnesses were gathered around—clergymen, nobles, and learned men! What a striking picture of the power of truth, however feeble the instrument by which it is conveyed!

Feckenham commenced as follows:

Feckenham.—Madam, I lament your heavy case, and yet I doubt not but that you bear out this heavy sorrow of yours with a constant and patient mind.

Lady Jane Grey.—You are welcome unto me, sir, if your coming be to give Christian exhortation. And as for my heavy case, I thank God, I do so little lament it, that rather I account the same for a more manifest declaration of God's favor towards me, than ever he showed me at any time before. And therefore there is no cause why either you or others, which bear me no good will, should lament or be grieved with this my case, being a thing so profitable for my soul's health.

F.—I am here come to you at this present

time to instruct you in the true doctrine of the right faith: although I have so great confidence in you, that I shall have, I trust, little need to travel with you much therein.

Jane.—Forsooth, I heartily thank the queen's highness, which is not unmindful of her humble subject; and I hope, likewise, that you no less will do your duty therein, both truly and faithfully, according to that you were sent for.

F.—What is then required of a Christian man?

Jane.—That he should believe in God the Father, the Son, and the Holy Ghost, three persons and one God.

F.—What, is there nothing else to be required or looked for in a Christian, but to believe in him?

Jane.—Yes, we must love him with all our heart, and all our soul, and with all our mind, and our neighbor as ourself.

F.—Why, then, faith neither justifieth, nor saveth.

Jane.—Yes, verily, faith, as St. Paul saith, only justifieth.

F.—Why, St. Paul saith, If I have all faith without love, it is nothing.

17

Jane.—True it is; for how can I love him whom I trust not? Or how can I trust him whom I love not? Faith and love go both together, and yet love is comprehended in faith.

F.—How shall we love our neighbor?

Jane.—To love our neighbor, is to feed the hungry, to cloth the naked, and give drink to the thirsty, and to do to him as we would do to ourselves.

F.—Why, then it is necessary unto salvation, to do good works also, and it is not sufficient only to believe.

Jane.—I deny that, and I affirm that faith only saveth; but it is meet for a Christian, in token that he followeth his master Christ, to do good works, yet may we not say that they profit to our salvation. For when we have done all, yet we are unprofitable servants, and faith only in Christ's blood saveth us.

F.—How many sacraments are there?

Jane.—Two: the one the sacrament of baptism, and the other the sacrament of the Lord's supper.

F.—No, there are seven.

Jane.—By what scripture find you that?

F.—Well, we will talk of that hereafter. But what is signified by your two sacraments?

Jane.—By the sacrament of baptism I am washed with water, and regenerated by the Spir·it, and that washing is a token to me that I am the child of God. The sacrament of the Lord's supper offered unto me, is a sure seal and testimony that I am, by the blood of Christ, which he shed for me on the cross, made partaker of the everlasting kingdom.

F.—Why, what do you receive in that sacrament? Do you not receive the very body and blood of Christ?

Jane.—No, surely, I do not so believe. I think that at the supper I neither receive flesh nor blood, but bread and wine; which bread, when it is broken, and the wine, when it is drank, putteth me in remembrance how that for my sins the body of Christ was broken, and his blood shed on the cross, and with that bread and wine, I receive the benefits that come by the breaking of his body and the shedding of his blood for our sins, on the cross.

F.—Why, doth not Christ speak these words: Take, eat; this is my body? Require you any plainer words? Doth he not say it is his body?

Jane.—I grant he saith so; and so he saith, I am the vine, I am the door; but he is never the more the door nor the vine. Doth not St. Paul say, He calleth things that are not, as though they were? God forbid that I should say, that I eat the very natural body and blood of Christ: for then, either I should pluck away my redemption, or else there were two bodies, or two Christs. One body was tormented on the cross, and if they did eat another body, then had he two bodies; or, if his body were eaten, then it was not broken upon the cross; or, if it were broken upon the cross, it was not eaten of his disciples.

F.—Why? Is it not as possible that Christ, by his power, could make his body both to be eaten and broken, as to be born of a woman without seed of man, and to walk upon the sea, having a body, and other such like miracles as he wrought by his power only?

Jane.—Yes, verily, if God would have done at his supper any miracles, he might have done so: but I say, that when he minded no work nor miracles, but only to break his body, and shed his blood on the cross for our sins. But I pray you to answer me this one question ·

Where was Christ when he said, Take, eat; this is my body? Was he not at the table when he said so? He was at that time alive, and suffered not till the next day. What took he but bread? what brake he but bread? and what gave he but bread? Look, what he took he brake; and look, what he brake he gave; and look, what he gave, they did eat : and yet all this while he himself was alive, and at supper before his disciples; or else they were deceived.

F.—You ground your faith upon such authors as say and unsay both in a breath, and not upon the church, to whom you ought to give credit.

Jane.—No, I ground my faith on God's word, and not upon the church; for if the church be a good church, the faith of the church must be tried by God's word, and not God's word by the church, nor yet my faith. Shall I believe the church because of antiquity? or shall I give credit to the church that taketh away from me the half part of the Lord's supper, and will not let any man receive it in both kinds? which things, if they deny to us, then deny they to us a part of our salvation. And I say that it is an evil church, and not the spouse of Christ, but the spouse of the devil, that altereth the Lord's supper, and both taketh from it and addeth to it. To that church (say I) God will add plagues, and from that church will he take their part out of the book of life. Do they learn that of St. Paul, when he ministered to the Corinthians in both kinds? Shall I believe this church? God forbid.

F.—That was done for a good intent of the church, to avoid an heresy that sprang up from it.

Jane.—Why? shall the church alter God's will and ordinance for good intent? How did King Saul? The Lord God defend.

The conversation proceeded in like manner, but to no purpose. When Feckenham took his leave he said:

F.—I am sorry for you; for I am sure that we two shall never more meet.

Jane.—True it is, that we shall never meet, except God turn your heart. For I am assured unless you repent and turn to God, you are in an evil case: and I pray God, in the bowels of his mercy, to send you his Holy Spirit: for he hath given you his great gift of utterance, if it pleased him also to open the eyes of your heart.

Throughout the whole discussion Lady Jane

conducted herself with the utmost calmness and meekness; indeed her witnesses were astonished at her deportment, as well as by her vigor of mind and language. She has left somewhere among her books, the following lines in refer- ence to this discussion :

"Mr. Feckenham gave me a long, tedious, yet eloquent reply, using many strong and logical persuasions to compel me to have leaned to their church; but my faith hath armed my resolution to withstand any assault that words could then use against me. Of many other articles of re- ligion we reasoned; but those formerly rehearsed were the chiefest and most effectual.

"JANE DUDLEY."

The day had now arrived which at first had been designated as the time for the execution of Lady Jane and her husband. There had been a respite granted, but Lady Jane refused to ac- cept it; but despite her refusal, the council post- poned her execution until the 12th of February. On the 10th, the wretched Duke of Suffolk was brought to the Tower a prisoner, but it is sup- posed that his daughter, Lady Jane, knew no- thing of his arrest, for on the evening previous

she addressed to him a celebrated letter, which
follows. The Duke was thus brought to become
a witness of his daughter's dreadful fate; and
unless his heart was turned to stone, it must
have been filled with pain and remorse at the
sight of that fair, young girl, offered up upon
the scaffold as a sacrifice, to expiate his own
blunders or ambitious acts. For his sake
alone, or the sake of his friends, she had consented to act the part she did, and now she was
receiving the penalty. It is, however, improper
to say that she consented to the usurpation, for
she never acquiesced in the plans of Northumberland and her father. She was literally *forced*
to accept the crown, and would have been pardoned for the treason had her father not a
second time transgressed the laws of the nation,
and attempted to rally a few uneasy men in the
provinces around her name,—she all the time
the unoffending and innocent inmate of a prison,
—and thus ensure her destruction! But at last
the Duke of Suffolk was in prison, from which
he never was to depart, but to walk up the steps
of a scaffold. Here in his dungeon his heart
could not have tasted the peace which diffused
a radiance over the countenance of his daughter,

like the aureola of glory around the brow of an
angel! How sadly must her letter have come
to him—how full it must have been of reproof—
and yet how tender and kind it is! The following is a copy:

"LETTER FROM LADY JANE TO HER FATHER.

"Father,—

"Although it hath pleased God to hasten
my death by you, by whom my life should
rather have been lengthened, yet can I so patiently take it, as yield more hearty thanks for
shortening my woful days, than if the whole
world had been given unto my possession, with
life lengthened at my own will. And albeit I
am well assured of your impatient griefs, re-
doubled manifold ways, both in bewailing your
own woe, and especially, as I hear, my unfortunate state; yet my dear father, if I may without
offence rejoice in my own mishaps, meseems in
this I may account myself blessed, that washing
my hands in the innocency of my fact, my guiltless blood may cry before the Lord, mercy to
the innocent. And yet though I must needs
acknowledge, that being constrained, and as you
wot well enough, continually assayed, in taking

upon'me I seemed to consent, and therein grievously offended the queen and her laws; yet do
I assuredly trust, that this my offence towards
God is so much the less, in that being in so royal
estate as I was, my enforced honor blended
never with mine innocent heart: and thus, good
father, I have opened unto you the state wherein I at present stand. Whose death at hand,
although to you, perhaps, it may seem right
woful, to me there is nothing that can be more
welcome, than from this vale of misery to aspire
to that heavenly throne of all joy and pleasure,
with Christ our Saviour. In whose steadfast
faith, if it may be lawful for the daughter so to
write to the father, the Lord that hitherto hath
strengthened you, so continue you, that at the
last we may meet in heaven with the Father,
the Son, and the Holy Ghost.   JANE."

It is not known when this letter was received
by the Duke of Suffolk, but probably the day
before the execution of his meek daughter. Nor
is any mention made by any historian of those
times of which we write, of the effect it had
upon his mind.

The lieutenant of the Tower at this time was

Sir John Gage, and having many opportunities of seeing Lady Jane and her husband, he could not help loving them, and desired not only to testify his respect and affection for them, but wished also to secure some token of their esteem for him, which he could keep in their memory. He therefore presented them a small book, bound in vellum, consisting of the devotions of an English Protestant of noble blood, who was wrongfully cast into prison. By some the book was supposed to have been written by the Duke of Somerset, and that the last five prayers in the volume were added by him on his second imprisonment, which ended in his execution. Upon this book, on the margin, Lady Jane wrote two notes,—one to her father, and one to Sir John Gage,—and Lord Guildford wrote one to his father-in-law, which was as follows:

" Your loving and obedient son wisheth unto your grace long life in this world, with as much joy and comfort as ever I wished to myself; and in the world to come joy everlasting.

" Your most humble son, till death,

" G. DUDLEY."

A few pages further on, upon the margin of a leaf, is the following note from Lady Jane Grey to her father:

"The Lord comfort your grace, and that in his word, wherein all creatures only are to be comforted.   And though it hath pleased God to take away two of your children, yet think not, I most humbly beseech your grace, that you have lost them; but trust that we, by leaving this mortal life, have now an immortal life. And I, for my part, as I have honored your grace in this life, will pray for you in another life.   Your always humble daughter,

"JANE DUDLEY."

To Sir John Gage, Lady Jane addressed the following note, on the margin of the same book:

"Forasmuch as you have desired so simple a woman to write in so worthy a book, good master lieutenant, therefore I shall, as a friend, desire you, and as a Christian require you, to call upon God to incline your heart to his laws, to quicken you in his way, and not to take the words of truth utterly out of your mouth.   Live still to die, that by death you may purchase eternal life ; and remember the end of Methusaleh, who, as we read in the Scriptures, was the longest liver that was of a man, died at the last. For as the preacher saith, there is a time to be born and a time to die, and the day of death is better than the day of our birth.

"Yours, as the Lord knoweth, as a friend,

"JANE DUDLEY."

The following day—the 11th of February— Lady Jane was constantly absorbed in meditation and prayer. In the evening she read the New Testament in Greek. After reading for a while she closed the book, then taking it up again and looking at the end of it, she saw some blank leaves, and taking pen and ink, wrote an exhortation to her sister Katharine. When she had finished it, she delivered the book to Mistress Ellen, one of her attendants, asking her to bear it to her sister, as a last token of her love and remembrance.

It is as follows :

"Good Sister Katharine,—

"I have here sent you a book, which, although it be not outwardly trimmed with gold,

yet inwardly is more worth than precious stones.
It is the book, dear sister, of the law of the
Lord.   It is his testament and last will, which
he bequeathed unto us wretches; which shall
lead you to the path of eternal joy; and if you,
with a good mind to read it, and with an earnest mind do purpose to follow it, it shall bring
you to an immortal and everlasting life. It shall
teach you to live, and learn you to die. It shall
win you more than you should have gained by
the possession of your woful father's lands. For
as, if God had prospered him, you should have
inherited his lands; so if you apply diligently
this book, seeking to direct your life after it, you
shall be an inheritor of such riches, as neither
the covetous shall withdraw from you, neither
they shall steal, neither yet the moths corrupt.   Desire with David, good sister, to understand the law of the Lord God. Live still to
die, that you, by death, may purchase eternal
life.   And trust not that the tenderness of your
age shall lengthen your life; for as soon, if God
calls, goeth the young as the old; and labor
always to learn to die. Defy the world, deny
the devil, despise the flesh, and delight yourself
only in the Lord. Be penitent for your sins,

and yet despair not: be strong in faith, and yet presume not; and desire with St. Paul, to be dissolved, and to be with Christ, with whom, even in death, there is life. Be like the good servant, and even at midnight waking, lest when death cometh and stealeth upon you as a thief in the night, you be with the evil servant, found sleeping: and lest for lack of oil, you be found like the five foolish women, and like him that had not on the wedding garment, and then ye be cast out from the marriage. Rejoice in Christ as I do. Follow the steps of your master, Christ, and take up your cross: lay your sins on his back, and always embrace him. And as touching my death, rejoice as I do, good sister, that I shall be delivered of this corruption, and put on incorruption. For I am assured that I shall, for losing a mortal life, win an immortal life, the which I pray God grant you, and send you his grace to live in his fear, and to die in the true Christian faith, from the which, in God's name I exhort you, that you never swerve, neither for hope of life, nor for fear of death. For if you will deny his truth to lengthen your life, God will deny you, and shorten your days. And if you cleave unto him, he will prolong your days to your comfort and his glory. To which glory God bring me now, and you hereafter, when it pleaseth him to call you. Fare you well, good sister, and put your only trust in God, who only must help you. JANE."

This striking letter was written the night before she was executed. The solemn shades of evening enveloped her apartment in the Tower, and she well knew that the morning light would come only to guide her feet to the scaffold! As a token of the state of her mind in the immediate prospect of death, this letter is exceedingly interesting. The Testament in which it was written still is preserved in England.

It would seem as if Mary would have allowed her cousin to remain in quiet the last night before her death; but no, the moment Lady Jane had finished her beautiful exhortation to her sister, two bishops and two learned doctors stood at the door of her apartments, seeking admission. They entered, and for two long hours endeavored to persuade her to recant, and die in the bosom of the Catholic church. And this when her hours on earth were but few, and she

had begged them to go their way, and let her
rest in quiet. It may have been that nothing
but zeal was the cause for this persecution, but
it strikes us that one cause was anger at Lady
Jane's perseverance in her belief in Protestantism, and her wonderful calmness in view of
death. The terrible efforts of her enemies to convert her to Catholicism, look to us as if caused
by something else than mere religious zeal.
There was a kind of gratification in seeing her
obliged to answer all the difficult questions
which the cool and calculating priests could
put to her, in worrying the poor creature's last
hours, as the deer is worried by the ravenous
hounds. But it was impossible to disturb her
peaceful spirit, " for her faith being built upon
the rock Christ, was by no worldly persuasion
or comfort to be either moved or shaken ; so
that after the expense of time, and the loss of
much speech, they left her (as they said) a lost
and forsaken member : but she, as before, prayed
for them, and with a most charitable patience
endured their worst censures." So writes a
faithful historian of her times.

At length the theological disputants left her
alone. It must now have been late in the even-

1

ing, but Lady Jane, as soon as her visitors left, sat down to the composition of a prayer which had solaced her in prison. She wrote it out and corrected it, and it has been carefully preserved to this day. It is as follows:

"A PRAYER MADE BY LADY JANE IN THE TIME OF HER TROUBLE.

"O Lord, thou God and father of my life, hear me, poor and desolate woman, which flieth unto thee only, in all troubles and miseries. Thou, O Lord, art the only defender and deliverer of those that put their trust in thee; and therefore, I being defiled with sin, encumbered with affliction, unquieted with troubles, wrapt in cares, overwhelmed with miseries, vexed with temptations, and grievously tormented with long imprisonment of this vile mass of clay, my sinful body, do come unto thee, O merciful Saviour, craving thy mercy and help, without which so little hope of deliverance is left, that I may utterly despair of any liberty. Albeit it is expedient that, seeing our life standeth upon trying. we should be visited sometime with some adversity, whereby we might both be tried

whether we be of the flock or no, and also
know thee and ourselves the better; yet thou
that saidst thou wouldst not suffer us to be
tempted above our power, be merciful unto
me now, a miserable wretch, I beseech thee,
humbly desiring thee that I may neither be
too much puffed up with prosperity, neither
too much pressed down with adversity, lest I,
being too full, should deny thee, my God, or
being too low brought, should despair, and blas-
pheme thee, my Lord and Saviour. O merciful God, consider my misery best known unto
thee; and be thou now unto me a strong tower
of defence, I humbly require thee. Suffer me
not to be tempted above my power; but either
be thou deliverer unto me out of this great
misery, or else give grace patiently to bear thy
heavy hand and sharp correction. It was thy
right hand that delivered the people of Israel
out of the hands of Pharaoh, which for the
space of four hundred years did oppress them,
and keep them in bondage. Let it, therefore,
likewise seem good to thy fatherly goodness, to
deliver me, a sorrowful wretch, for whom thy
son Christ shed his precious blood on the cross,
out of this miserable captivity and bondage

wherein I am now.   How long wilt thou be
absent?   Forever?   O Lord, hast thou forgotten to be gracious, and hast thou shut up thy
loving kindness in displeasure?   Wilt thou be
no more entreated?   Is thy mercy clean gone
forever, and thy promise come utterly to an
end forever more?   Why dost thou make so
long tarry?   Shall I despair of thy mercy, O
God?   Far be that from me.   I am thy work-
manship, created in Christ Jesus; give me grace,
therefore, to tarry thy leisure, and patiently
to bear thy works, assuredly knowing that
as thou canst, thou wilt deliver me, when it
shall please thee, nothing doubting or mistrust-
ing thy goodness towards me: for thou knowest better what is good for me than I do:
therefore do with me, in all things, what thou
wilt, and plague me what way thou wilt.   Only
in the mean time arm me, I beseech thee, with
thy armor, that I may stand fast, my loins being
girded about with verity, having on thy breast-
plate of righteousness, and shod with the shoes
prepared by the gospel of peace; above all
things taking to me the shield of faith, where-
with I may be able to quench all the fiery
darts of the wicked, and taking the helmet of

salvation, and the sword of the spirit, which is thy most holy word, praying always, with all manner of prayer and supplication, that I may refer myself wholly to thy will, abiding thy pleasure, and comforting myself in those troubles that it shall please thee to send me ; seeing such troubles be profitable for me, and seeing I am assuredly persuaded that it cannot be but well all that thou dost. Hear me, O merciful Father, for His sake whom thou wouldst should be a sacrifice for my sins: to whom, with Thee and the Holy Ghost, be all honor and glory. Amen."

The feeling of the people in reference to the execution of Lady Jane Grey and Lord Guildford Dudley, was intense. Sympathy for them was expressed everywhere ; and, indeed, the city of London was, from this and many other causes, in a state of panic. Military law prevailed, and fifty soldiers, who had deserted the queen's standard, were hung. They were all citizens of London, and were hung before their own doors. Corpses were to be seen in every street, and in every house in London there was fear and agitation. And now came the morning of Lady Jane Grey's execution.   The Twelfth day of February, 1554, is a day long to be re-membered by students of English history, for on that day perished one of the loveliest and most innocent and gentle of all heroines.   The month of February is generally in England a chilly and stormy month, and we may well suppose that little beauty of nature was visible that day ; so sad were the events then tran-. spiring, that it would hardly have been meet for nature to be arrayed in her most attractive robes.

Queen Mary at first intended that Lady Jane and her husband should be executed to-gether on Tower Hill.   What could have been her reason for wishing them to die together we know not, but it certainly was a very cruel thought.   However, such was the universal and strong feeling in favor of the unfortunate pair, that the council, fearing that were the people to see the death of Lady Jane, it would add fuel to the fires of agitation still raging in the city, countermanded the first order, and directed that Lord Guildford Dudley should suffer alone on the Tower Hill, and that Lady Jane Grey should be executed within the walls of the prison, and of course out of sight of the compassionate people.

Lord Guildford was soon informed of this change in the attendant ceremonies of the execution, and was exceedingly anxious for an interview with his wife. The queen was quite willing that he should be gratified in his wish, well knowing that it could only add to the anguish of them both, and tend to discompose their minds. Lady Jane was, however, sufficiently prudent and courageous to refuse to see her husband. She well knew that their meeting must be agonizing, full of bitter tears and pain, and that after such a scene neither would be so calm and so well prepared to meet triumphantly the death which awaited them. She sent back word to her husband that the tenderness of their parting would overcome the fortitude of both, and would too much unbend their minds from that constancy which their approaching end required of them. Their separation, she said, would only be for a moment; and that they would soon rejoin each other, in a country where their affections would be forever united, and where death, disappointment, and misfortunes could no longer have access to them, or disturb their eternal felicity!

A more beautiful reply could not have been given, nor a wiser decision made. Indeed, throughout the whole career of this angelic creature, we are constantly surprised at her wisdom, as well as gentleness. Though tender in years, constitution, and disposition, yet she ever manifests the superior wisdom of age. This is not mere panegyric—the reader has seen how circumspectly Lady Jane conducted herself at court amid every temptation, and how pure she came from it; has seen how prudently she ever carried herself, how learned she was, and still how lovely. There was only one mistake—the acceptance of the crown—and it never can properly be said that she *accepted* it. Such was the amount of persuasion and force used against her better feelings and decisions, that she was scarcely a free agent in the act of the usurpation of the crown. Every other act of her life recorded in history, redounds to her glory as a wise, truly affectionate, and pious woman.

But we must hasten to describe the solemn events of the memorable Twelfth. Soon after Lady Jane Grey sent the communication just alluded to, to Lord Guildford, he was led out of the Tower. When he was outside of the gate, he was given up to the custody of one of the sheriffs of London, named Thomas Offleie. When passing out to the gate, he walked immediately beneath the window of Lady Jane, and for a moment he gazed up at her with a look of sad-ness yet of affection. She caught his eye, and gave him a signal that she saw him, and that he yet reigned over her heart. When he was out of sight, she resumed her seat, and with perfect calmness and resignation awaited the dread hour of death. She had seen the last of her living husband—in a few minutes more he would be in eternity!

When Lord Guildford arrived at the gate, many of his friends were there waiting for him, and he shook hands tenderly with Sir Anthony Bronne, John Throckmorton, and many others, bidding them farewell with calmness, and ask-ing them to pray for him. When he approached the scaffold, he mounted it with dignified com-posure, and knelt down in silent prayer to God. It is said after he had been on his knees for a few moments, he paused, and raised his eyes and hands up to Heaven, while a single tear dropped from his eye. A large crowd of people were gathered about the place, and he spoke to them, desiring that they would pray for him; then he quietly laid his head down upon the block, and gave himself up to the executioner. The axe fell—and he was dead.

His head was laid in a white cloth, and with the body carried to a cart, in which they were taken back to the Tower for burial. News of his courage and noble conduct in death flew to Lady Jane Grey, and she was comforted. She was sitting quietly in her chamber, surrounded by her attendants, when the rumbling of a cart was heard. Lady Jane rose at once and walked to the window. Her attendants endeavored to keep her back, for they knew that in the cart were the remains of her husband; but she overcame them with dignity, and passed to the window, and looked steadily down upon the lifeless form of her loved husband. The sight must have given her an awful shock, but the only sign she exhibited was a deep, long sigh, and the following apostrophe, which burnt from her almost broken though calm heart:

"Oh! Guildford! Guildford! the antepast is not so bitter that you have tasted, and that I shall soon taste, as to make my flesh tremble; but that is nothing compared to the feast that you and I shall this day partake of in Heaven!"

But now her own time had come. Preparations had been making inside the walls of the Tower for her execution, a scaffold being erected upon a green opposite to the White Tower. When all was ready, the lieutenaut of the Tower, Sir John Gage, asked if she would not, before she left her apartments, give to him a small present, which he might keep always as a memorial of her. She gave him a table book, where she had just written three sentences—one in Greek, one in Latin, and one in English—upon her husband's dead body. The meaning of these sentences was that human justice was against his body, but that divine mercy would save his soul; that if her own fault deserved punishment, yet her youth at least, and her imprudence, were worthy of excuse, and that God and posterity would show her favor.

In her chamber she scratched the following with a pin:

> "Deo juvante, nil nocet . . . . . malus;
> Et non juvante, nil juvat labor gravis.
> Post tenebris, spero lucem."

These lines have been translated as follows.

> "Whilst God assists us, Envy bites in vain;
> If God forsake us, fruitless all our pain.
>   I hope for light after darkness."

Four more lines, the following, it is said were also written by her:

> " Whate'er by man, as mortal, is assigned,
> Should raise compassion, reader, in thy mind!
> Mourn others' woes, and to thy own resign;
> The fate which I have found, may soon be thine."

Lady Jane, being told that everything was ready for her execution, arose, and accompanied by her attendants, walked to the scaffold. Her countenance was natural and happy; not a single tear was in her eyes, nor scarcely a shade of sorrow upon her countenance. Her two maids, or attendants, Elizabeth Tilney and Mistress Ellen, wept aloud, but their sweet mistress was serene and beautiful as a summer morning. When she was come down from Master Partridge's home, where her apartments were, she was delivered into the hands of the London sheriffs, and her conduct was so modest, and yet so fearless, without agitation or curiosity, that every one was surprised. As a striking writer has said, "like a divine body, going to be united to her heart's best and longest beloved, so showed she forth all the beams of a well-mixed and well-tempered alacrity, rather instructing patience how it should suffer, than being by patience any way able to endure the the travail of so grievous a journey."

The lieutenant offered her his hand to lead her forth, and she took it without the slightest symptom of fear, without any paleness of cheek, and without a tear. While she was walking to the scaffold, she held in her hand a book, by the help of which she prayed very fervently, though Feckenham accompanied her, and endeavored to interrupt her in her devotions. She ascended the scaffold as naturally as if she had been mounting the stairs of her own chamber, and stood meekly before her murderers until there was silence, when she spoke to the people present as follows, in a clear and pleasant voice:

" Good people, I come hither to die, and by a law I am condemned to the same. My offence against the queen's highness was only in consent to the device of others, which is now deemed treason; but it was never of my seeking, but by counsel of those who would seem to have further understanding of such things than I, who

knew little of the law, and much less of the titl,s
to the crown. The fact, indeed, was unlawful,
and the consenting thereto by me, or in my behalf. I do wash my hands thereof in innocence,
before God and you, good Christian people, this
day." When she pronounced these words Lady
Jane wrung her hands, some thought from agony
of mind, but it was undoubtedly an action to
illustrate her words. She went on with perfect
composure to say, "I pray you all, good Christian people, to bear me witness, that I die a true
Christian woman, and that I look to be saved
by none other means but only by the mercy of
God, and the merits of the blood of his only
son, Jesus Christ; and I confess when I did
know the word of God, I neglected the same,
and loved myself and the world, and therefore
this plague and punishment is happily and wor-
thily happened unto me for my sins; and yet I
thank God of his goodness, that he has thus
given me time and respite to repent. And now,
good people, while I am alive, I pray you to
assist me with your prayers."

Lady Jane was surrounded by Catholic divines; not a single Protestant clergyman was
allowed to be with her during her last moments;

and in her speech she seems to have determined to let the world know that she died in the Protestant faith. Perhaps she was afraid that they would attempt to make her out a convert to Catholicism, so strenuous had been their exertions to that end ; and therefore her dying speech set at rest, at once and forever, the question.

When she was through speaking she knelt down to pray, and seeing Feckenham at her side, she pointed at a psalm in her book, and meekly asked :

" Shall I say this psalm ? "

His reply was a simple "Yea;" and Lady Jane repeated the *Miserere mei Deus* in English, and in a solemn manner. When she had repeated this psalm, she said to Feckenham :

"God will abundantly requite you, good sir, for your humanity to me, though your discourses gave me more uneasiness than all the terrors of my approaching death."

Her devotions were now ended, and she was ready for the sacrifice of her life. She arose from her knees, still calm and beautiful, and began to undress, first taking off her gloves, and then her handkerchief, which articles she handed to Elizabeth Tilney, her maid. A book, which heretofore she had held in her hand, she now gave to the lieutenant's brother, Mr. Thomas Brydges.

She was proceeding to unloose her gown, when the executioner, meaning no harm, somewhat rudely attempted to assist her, but she mildly requested that he would not touch her; and turning to her maids, Elizabeth and Ellen, asked them to assist her. Her gown was unloosed and taken off, and then her "froze peste and handkerchief." When this was done, her maids gave her a white handkerchief, with which it was expected she would bandage her eyes.

The executioner, who seems to have been touched by her gentle behavior, and perhaps feared that she was offended with him for his attempt to assist her in unrobing, now knelt at her feet and asked her forgiveness for what he had done and was about to do, which she accorded to him in the sweetest manner. The executioner then rose up and asked her to stand upon some straw. In doing so she caught her first glance at the fearful fatal block. But it is said that she did not shrink from, nor show any fear of it, but said simply to the executioner:

"I pray you dispatch me quickly."

After saying this she knelt down and asked:

"Will you take it off before I lay me down?"

The executioner answered,

"No, madam."

Lady Jane now, without any apparent agitation, took with her own beautiful hands the white handkerchief, which we have before alluded to, and tied it carefully over her eyes. She was now blindfolded, and endeavored to feel for the block, and asked, "What shall I do? Where is it?"

A person near her, on the scaffold, guided her to the block, and she instantly laid her head upon it, and then, stretching her body out gracefully, rested for a moment, then exclaimed:

"Lord, into thy hands I commend my spirit!"

There was a moment of appalling silence—then the axe fell, and her lovely head rolled away from the body.

It is said that scarcely one of the spectators witnessed her death without tears, and many cried aloud. Even the hard-hearted priests who came to enjoy her agony, could not refrain from

M

19

weeping, and the good-hearted, though bigoted Feckenham, was filled with anguish.

Fuller declares that "it is reported that Lady Jane was as ladies wish to be who love their lords," when she was executed, and adds, "it was cruelty to cut down the tree with blossoms on it; and that which has saved the lives of many women, hastened her death; but God only knows the truth thereof." We know not what cause Fuller had for his remark, as no historian mentions any such fact or report.

Judge Morgan, so Fox writes, who sentenced Lady Jane to death, shortly after her execution went mad, and in his raving, constantly shouted the name of Lady Jane Grey, and asked to have her taken away from him; and so his life ended. It is not strange that the scene of her execution, which perhaps he was a witness of, should haunt the wretched man; that the saint-like person of Lady Jane, whom he had so unjustly consigned to an early death, should refuse to quit the chambers of his diseased mind, when upon his death-bed. There was a feeling everywhere abroad, which accused Mary and her council of cruelty in the execution of Lady Jane Grey, and time has strengthened that feeling, until at this day no one will attempt for a moment to justify her terrible act. There was really not the slightest danger to her crown from the continued existence of Lady Jane; and we think that though she may have been alarmed by her council, by representations of the insurrectionary state of the kingdom, yet one of the truest reasons why she signed the death-warrant was that, after all, she hated her cousin, as there is the best of evidence that she had done many years before. Lady Jane Grey's father and friends had been guilty of assisting in the degradation of the queen's mother and herself, and the claims of Lady Jane to the throne was without validity, unless Mary was declared to be of illegitimate birth. The queen could never overlook these facts—nor could Elizabeth, who reigned after her, and who, alike with Mary, was illegitimated by Northumberland and Suffolk in their state papers.

But when the innocent Lady Jane had expiated her mistake on the scaffold, it must have been that occasionally her memory rendered the pillow of the queen less fraught with pleasant dreams than it would have been, had Lady Jane Grey never perished by her hand. In the silent watches of the night, she must have some times seen the innocent girl's blood upon that pillow. One thing is very certain, that never afterward does she seem to have been happy; and she expired at last under circumstances of gloom and sadness.

CHAPTER. XIII.

HAVING concluded our narrative of the career
of Lady Jane Grey,—her childhood, marriage,
queenhood, and death,—little remains to be said.
A few words, however, will be necessary, to
sketch the fortunes of those persons who were
intimately connected with our heroine.

The Duke of Suffolk, Lady Jane's father,
when taken into custody by the queen's officers,
acted like a child, crying and moaning over
his fate. Five days after the execution of his
glorious child, he was himself brought to trial at
Westminster Hall. He was indicted for levying
war against the queen, and adhering to the
cause of Sir Thomas Wyatt, in order to depose
the queen, and set the crown upon the head of
his daughter.

m

He answered, that it was not treason for a peer of the realm, which he was, to raise his power and make his proclamation to avoid strangers out of the land making allusion to the Spaniards. The judges replied that he had done more; that he had opposed the queen's lieutenant at the head of her majesty's forces, which could not be construed as aught but high treason. He replied that he knew not that the person he opposed was the queen's lieutenant; that his brother had advised him to go down into the country, where he would be safe among his tenants; but if he staid in town, he would be committed to the Tower again.

The duke was condemned to death, and very justly, too, we think; for he had committed treason for the *second* time, and that, too, with the utmost recklessness of character. When he returned from Westminster Hall, the duke was very sad, and desired all the persons whom he met to pray for him. Six days afterward, on the twenty-third day of February, he was brought to the place of execution on Tower Hill, where he confessed that his sentence was a just one, because he had been disloyal to Queen Mary. He asked the people who were gathered to witness his death, to take warning from his fate, and be dutiful to the government. He avowed himself a believer in the Christian religion, and hoped for eternal mercy through Christ. After saying this, he was beheaded.

Sir Thomas Wyatt met his fate on the 11th of April; and a fortnight after, Lord Thomas Grey, brother to the late Duke of Suffolk, was beheaded on Tower Hill. At this time, Elizabeth, afterwards so renowned, was herself a prisoner, and in the same prison with her was Robert Dudley, brother to Guildford Dudley, Lady Jane Grey's husband. This person afterwards became the celebrated Earl of Leicester, and was Queen Elizabeth's favorite. By some it is asserted that the queen began to love him at this time, when they were in prison together. The Duchess of Suffolk survived her husband and her daughter for many years, dying in the year 1563. She married again, but her second husband was a gentleman much beneath her in social position; but it is suggested that she married low purposely, that she might be over-looked, and allowed to live out her remaining days in security. Her husband's name was Adrian Stokes, and for many years he was one of her family domestics. There was little in her character which can command our respect, though perhaps she was the equal of her husband

Of Lady Jane Grey's two sisters, Lady Katharine and Lady Mary, but little is known. Lady Katharine had been betrothed to Lord Herbert, son of the Earl of Pembroke, but he repudiated the engagement for political reasons, now that the name of Suffolk was covered with disgrace. Lady Katharine was thus most shamefully deserted. Fuller says quaintly of her:

" This Heraclita, or Lady of Lamentation, thus repudiated, was seldom seen with dry eyes for some years together, sighing out her sorrowful condition ; so that though the roses in her cheeks looked very wan and pale, it was not for want of watering."

During the reign of Elizabeth, the Lady Katharine fell in love with Edward Seymour, Earl of Hertford. They were married secretly ; but one day the queen discovered that Lady Katharine was *enciente*, and the secret came out that they had married without the queen's leave. Here was an excellent opportunity for Elizabeth to retaliate upon the daughter for the wrongs committed by her father many years before upon the queen, and she sent the couple to prison. Lady Katharine begged her friend, the Earl of Leicester,—brother to Lady Jane's husband,—to intercede in their behalf; but the earl dared not, for at that time he hoped to marry his queen, and cared not to remind her of his relationship to treasonable men. He therefore refused the suit of Katharine. In prison, the couple found means of access to each other, and in the course of time a second child was born, and a costly child it was to them, for the queen fined them £20,000. For seven long years she was confined to her dungeon, for the simple reason that she was a sister to the saint-like Lady Jane Grey. This was not the ostensible but the true reason for Elizabeth's outrageous cruelty. Lady Katharine, at the end of seven years, expired, worn down with grief and trouble.

Lady Mary Grey married a man of humble origin, purposely to escape the sad fate of her two sisters. She died childless in 1575.

When we contemplate the lessons which history affords us, the conviction becomes strong in our hearts—we cannot escape it if we would —that beyond this sphere of action there is a
m

Court, before which all personages, whether kings or peasants, must be tried, and where all the unrighteous verdicts rendered here will be over-ruled, and pure justice administered to all, without respect of persons.   It were easy to imagine before that judgment-throne the persons who have figured prominently in our pages—Henry VIII., covered with the blood of his victims—Queen Mary, earnest, but vindictive and cruel-hearted—and pure, spotless, glorious Lady Jane Grey!   We might go further, and decide, in our imaginations, the fate awaiting each—but we have no right.   God will judge righteously, and with Him we may trustingly confide the ministration of mercy and justice to our fellow-creatures and ourselves.

www.ingramcontent.com/pod-product-compliance
Lightning Source LLC
Chambersburg PA
CBHW021038030726
47496CB00006B/1588